32C, That's Me

'You can't always get what you want.'

That's what Mum said. She was wrong. Because
I had everything I wanted.
For a start I had the best family in the world.
Okay, my parents were pretty boring, married for ever,
you know the type, but actually I liked it that way and
anyway, I had the coolest sister. I also had a best mate
who was loyal and fun, plus, don't laugh, I even liked
school and my teachers.
And most important of all, I was going out with
Muggs and we were in love. Then we got the leading
roles in the school play, opposite each other.
It was the icing on my perfect cake.

'Pride comes before a fall.'

That's another of Mum's sayings. This time she
wasn't wrong. I always thought bad things happened
to other people, not me. I guess my luck had to
run out sooner or later . . .

32C, That's Me

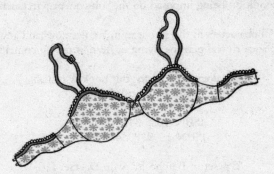

Chris Higgins

Hodder
Children's
Books

A division of Hachette Children's Books

A Catalogue record for this book is available
from the British Library

ISBN-10: 0 340 91727 X
ISBN-13: 9780340917275

Typeset in Bembo by Avon DataSet Ltd,
Bidford on Avon, Warwickshire

Printed and bound in Great Britain by Clays Ltd, St Ives plc

The paper and board used in this paperback by Hodder Children's
Books are natural recyclable products made from wood grown in
sustainable forests. The manufacturing processes conform to the
environmental regulations of the country of origin.

Hachette Children's Books
a division of Hodder Headline Ltd
338 Euston Road
London NW1 3BH

For Lucy, Claire, Pippa, Kate and Twig.

With thanks to Mel, Lindsey, Anne and Zöe

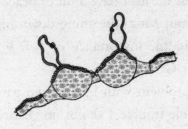

Step on a crack, you'll break your back.
Step on a line, you'll break your spine.

Every day, on my way home from school, I do this weird thing. As I turn into my street I recite this chant in my head and try to avoid the cracks in the pavement.

Me, superstitious? Never!

Well, okay, a bit.

Because, when I reach the last lamppost before our house, I take a deep breath and fill my lungs with air. You see, if I can get into the house without taking another breath, Mum won't be there.

I turn my key in the lock, lungs bursting. Nothing. No Radio 4, no voice on the phone, no dishes clattering in the kitchen.

My breath explodes in a big rush of air. Yes! Mum's not home yet. I have the house to myself.

Don't get me wrong, I don't hate my mum or anything. It just means I have a bit of peace to go on the Internet, without Mum breathing down my neck about homework and 'the importance of Year 9 in laying the foundation for GCSEs'.

That's the problem with having two parents who are teachers. Double trouble. I've got no chance.

Actually they're not that bad. Quite cool really, though I'd never admit that to them or anyone else.

I dump my bag on the floor and help myself to a Coke from the fridge and a couple of rice cakes. I'm really into them. 'Gluten-free', it says on the packet. That's Mum's influence. I just like the taste.

The light's flashing on the answerphone. It's a message from Ali. Scatty Ali. My best mate. We're as different as chalk and cheese, but we've been friends since reception class. She was away today.

'Hi, Jess. How was school? I've been doubled up in agony but I'm okay now. Can I copy your maths? Ring me.'

Trust Ali. Ever since she started her periods she has a day off each month with stomach-ache which miraculously disappears at 3.30. She gets away with it because she gets her mum to write a note. Dumb mum.

I'm just jealous. You have to be on your deathbed in this house before anyone's allowed to take a sicky.

Though, don't tell anyone, but actually I like school and don't want to miss it. Especially now I'm going out with Muggs. I wouldn't mind the odd day in bed though.

Chance'd be a fine thing.

You see, my dad's in charge of absences at my school. He's the deputy head and teaches me science as well. I had to do sex education with him in Year 7. How embarrassing is that? At least Mum has the sense to work in a different school.

The next message is for him, all about money and pensions. Boring. Dad's forever trying to work out if he can afford to retire early, though Mum and I think this is just a hobby of his. Every so often he flips into stress mode and goes off on how he'll have to keep working till he's sixty-five to support my sister and me through uni. As he's only forty-eight now, that's hardly likely, especially as Carly is nearly nineteen and will be starting at Bristol in September.

Gran's voice comes on next. My gran's wicked. It's the usual. She's forgotten how to set the video and the over-60s have got a salsa class on tonight she doesn't want to miss. Can Dad ring her back?

The last one's for Mum. Message for Mrs Diane Bayliss from the Daybreak Centre asking her to attend tomorrow at 2pm. Wonder what that's about?

Mum teaches life skills and special needs in her school

so it's probably something to do with that. I must remember to tell her. She never checks for messages. She's not exactly technically illiterate, but not far from it. For her, checking her mail is exactly that. She comes in and looks to see if there's any post for her and there never is because she leaves the boring brown envelopes for Dad to open. She's got an e-mail address that Carly set up for her before she left so they could keep in touch, but she hardly ever uses it.

That reminds me. I go into the dining room to check my e-mails. Yes! There's one from Carly. It's from Byron Bay in New South Wales, Australia. Carly, the Byron Siren.

Carly's having a gap year before uni. I really miss her. She flew to Bangkok after her A-level results last year and spent a few months in Thailand. Mum and Dad couldn't say anything because she'd got the grades she needed and that was the bargain they'd made. Work hard for your A-levels and then do what you want for a year.

Mind you, I reckon they wouldn't have stopped her if she'd failed them altogether. There's still an element of the old hippies in Mum and Dad, under that veneer of middle-class respectability. That's how they met, in the late 70s, on the hippy trail. Dad had been hitch-hiking to Turkey and Mum had been on her way back from Kathmandu with a jerk called Jeremy, and they met in Istanbul in the Pudding Shop. Mum ditched Jeremy and went off to live on a Greek island with Dad for a month, sleeping on beaches and on the roofs of houses. The rest is history, as they say.

Anyway, now Carly's having a whale of a time in sunny Australia. The e-mail says it all.

Met a gorgeous surfer dude called Todd. Todd the Bod! He is <u>seriously</u> sexy! How does 6 foot 4, sunbleached hair and great pecs grab you? And, guess what! Have got a job! Bad news is, it's waitressing. Good news is, it's at a café on the beach. So I'm topping up my suntan as I'm earning money and get to chat up all these fit guys at the same time!

This is all seriously good news for me as it's what I intend to be doing in four years' time. I type out a reply to her, telling her all the gossip, though there's not a lot going on.

Muggs and I are still together and it's getting better by the day. Kelly Harris hates me cos she's fancied him for ages. Think Ali's a bit jealous too. Guess what? Miss Taylor wants me to audition for the role of Lady Macbeth! Mum's worried I'll fall behind with my work. Ali's going for it as well but she's got no chance. Mum and Dad are boring as ever. I miss you.

Send.

I'm on the Internet looking up stuff about Lady Macbeth when Mum comes in. It's our Shakespeare text and Miss Taylor thinks we can make it come alive by putting it on ourselves. She's really cool like that, she's a great teacher. I'd so love to take the role of Lady Macbeth, she's such a nasty piece of work. I reckon I'm in with a chance as Miss usually picks me to read her in class because she says I make sense of the words.

That's down to Mum. She used to read aloud to Carly when she was breastfeeding me and she reckons I took it all in. I was reading properly before I started school. In reception Miss Barry put me with Ali to help her because she found reading hard. I've been doing Ali's work for her ever since.

Do you know something? Mum used to read Shakespeare to me in bed when I was little. I didn't know what she was on about but I loved being snuggled up next to her and listening to the sounds and patterns her voice made. Maybe that's why I love Shakespeare so much now.

Oh, and I forgot to mention, Muggs is going to try out for Macbeth. How romantic is that!

'Hiya, love. Had a good day? You're not in a chatroom are you?' Mum asks, all in one breath. Good old Mum, she doesn't even know what a chatroom is. She's just heard the phrase and thinks it's something mildly unsavoury.

'Yes, I'm just fixing a date with a fifty-year-old saddo

called Ronald who's pretending to be a fifteen-year-old called Dazza,' I answer.

'Well, don't stay on there all night, you've got your homework to do.' Mum's voice comes from the kitchen, where she's pulling out food from the freezer. She never listens when she gets home from school. It takes her till after tea to stop being a teacher and issuing orders.

'Spaghetti bolognese okay?'

'Fine,' I say, engrossed in the words on the screen. She has a really bad press, Lady Macbeth. According to this article, there's loads more to her than the scheming wife she's made out to be.

'Did your dad say if he was going to be late tonight?'

'Haven't a clue.' I'm intent on grabbing pages off the net about Lady Macbeth and her lack of power.

Mum starts pulling stuff out of the washing machine.

'Stick this on the line for me, Jess. It should dry before it's dark.'

'Mu–um! I'm doing my homework!'

It's a weird fact of life that Mum goes on all the time that I never do any homework but finds a million ways to stop me from actually doing any.

'Go on, Jess. It won't take you a minute. I want to get the tea on. I'm off to Stretch and Tone tonight.'

She's always doing something, Mum, she's never still for a minute. Dad's much more laid-back.

'You don't need to go anyway,' I grumble, picking up the basket of wet washing. Mum's got a great figure, something else I've inherited from her apparently. At least, that's what Carly says. She says I'm 'well-endowed' in the right places. She means I've got big boobs like Mum. Carly's a different shape all together. She's more like Dad – well, not really, because he's a bloke – but the same sort of lean body type without the paunch. I'm more curvy.

To tell the truth, I'm still getting used to my boobs. They've crept up on me in the last couple of years. I like them, but I'm getting to the stage where I hope they won't grow any more. Ali thinks I'm nuts. She says they're my best asset. She's saving up for a boob job because she says hers are like two fried eggs.

'Don't forget these.'

Mum chucks some underwear that's got stuck in the back of the machine into the basket.

'Those bras are no good for you, you know.'

Here she goes. I can feel my hackles rising.

'Don't look at me like that, Jess. You need some support or your breasts will sag. You should come with me to Marks and Sparks and be measured. These skimpy little things do nothing for you.'

'No way,' I protest. 'I'm not wearing a boulder-holder for anyone!'

No one can infuriate me like my mother. She's got it off to a fine art. And she's oblivious to it. She can bring me to boiling point in 1.5 seconds and leave me simmering there without even noticing.

Dad's late and Mum's clucking that she'll never get to exercise class if he doesn't hurry up because she needs the car. At last he comes in, plonking his briefcase down by my bag and loosening his tie. Mum's about to tell us to move them but changes her mind when she sees how tired he looks.

'Busy day?'

'Mmm.' He puts the kettle on and runs his fingers through his hair. It's going a bit thin on top. 'You?'

'You're not kidding, I'm exhausted,' she says and launches into a lengthy and complicated description of her talk to Year 7 boys on personal hygiene. Gross. The strange thing is that she seems full of energy after her day whereas Dad really does look tired and crumpled.

It's not till we're halfway through our spag bog that I remember the messages on the phone.

'Oops. Gran wanted you to explain to her how to set the video, Dad.'

'Again,' said Mum, darkly.

'It's too late now. She'll have gone out. And there's someone about pensions on the answerphone.'

Dad grunts.

'Oh, and Mum, the Daybreak Centre rang. You've got an appointment there tomorrow at two.'

'What?' Mum looks startled.

'There's a message on the answer machine,' I mumble, my mouth full of pasta.

'I wish you wouldn't do that!' Mum snaps, getting up from the table and stacking dishes even though Dad and I haven't finished.

'What?' I ask in surprise.

'Listen to my messages. They could be private, you know.'

Dad and I look at each other in amazement. Mum's logic never ceases to surprise. She's throwing plates into the sink as if she's a guest at a Greek wedding.

'It's an answerphone. For all of us,' I explain patiently.

'Oh you know what I mean,' mutters Mum. 'Anyway, you two can wash up. I've got things to do.'

'I thought you were going to Stretch and Tone,' I say.

'It's too late now. And I'm too busy. I've got a load of stuff to do for school.'

'Ofsted,' mouths Dad as she sweeps out of the kitchen and goes upstairs.

'PMT,' I reply, chucking him the tea towel. 'I'll wash, you wipe.'

The next morning Mum's back to normal, though she hadn't come back downstairs the night before. I guess she was marking books in her room, then she called down to say she was having a bath and an early night. She gives me a hug as I go out of the door.

'Good luck for the audition today.'

I hug her back and say goodbye. Ali's at the end of the road, period pains forgotten for another month. I run to catch her up. She's stuffing a Mars bar down her throat for breakfast. It's not fair. She lives on a diet of chocolate and chips but she's skinny as a rake and never gets spots.

'Got your maths?' She gives me a chocolatey grin as I hand over my book. 'You're a star,' she says and copies down my answers as she walks along. Mum would go ballistic if she saw her, but it's no skin off my nose.

Dad's left an hour ago. He has to be at school early to

sort out the registers. There's no way I'd go with him anyway, even if he left at a civilised time. It's embarrassing enough having him in the same school as me without advertising the fact by arriving with him.

Ali thinks I'm nuts. She reckons it's great having my dad as deputy head and plays up to him like mad. He's got a soft spot for her too. He's known her since she was a little kid and he used to tease her to bits and she loved it. I used to feel a bit jealous sometimes, but Mum said it was because she didn't have a dad of her own so I stopped minding. Mum's more critical of her. She worries that she'll lead me astray. No chance.

Muggs is waiting for me at the school gate with his nose in *Macbeth*, reading over Act 1, Scene 3 for today's audition. I still can't believe I'm going out with him. Muggs, christened David Morgan. He's tall with long dark hair that he wears tied back in a ponytail for school, and when he smiles his eyes crinkle and his mouth goes lopsided and he looks soooo sexy. Everyone fancies him. And the bonus is, he's in Year 10 so I get to use the Upper School common room as his invited guest. We got to know each other during last year's production of *Little Shop of Horrors*, and by Christmas we were a couple. He's my first (and hopefully my last) boyfriend.

'Hiya,' I say, and give him a peck on the cheek. 'How's it going?'

He strikes a pose and looks Ali and me up and down and says:

> 'What are these,
> So withered and so wild in their attire,
> That look not like the inhabitants o'th'earth,
> And yet are on't?'

'Ha, ha, very funny,' I say, impressed despite myself. Ali looks at him as if he's mad. This is typical Muggs; he's probably stayed up half the night learning all of Act 1 so he'll be word-perfect for the audition.

I just don't get him. His home life's chaotic, with loads of little step and half-brothers and sisters, and parents who wouldn't notice in a month of Sundays whether he's done his homework or not, and he just gets on with it. He's good at everything – rugby, football, schoolwork, drama, the lot – and he's dead popular as well. I know my Dad rates him, which makes life a lot easier for us.

'What's he on about?' asks Ali. Shakespeare is not her strong point even though she's desperate for a leading role in the play.

'Speak if you can: what are you?' Muggs continues, putting his arms around me. I nestle close to him. I can feel his heart through his sweatshirt.

'Hail,' I say.

'Hail,' he answers.

'Lesser than Macbeth, and greater,' I continue.

'Not so happy, yet much happier,' he caps me, nuzzling my neck.

'You two are weird,' says Ali.

We both laugh and he gives me a kiss on the lips. My heart pounds. Next to me, Ali is giving Sean Wheeler from Muggs's class a full-on snog. She pulled him on Saturday night, not because she likes him but because he's an entrance ticket into the common room. Boys are always buzzing round her like bees round the proverbial honeypot. She's such a flirt. There's no way I'd snog Muggs in front of everyone even though I fancy him to death.

'Teachers,' warns Muggs, and Ali and Sean spring apart. He's spotted my dad on duty in the playground but it's okay, he's crouching down, talking to Miss Taylor through the window of her car. When he stands up he opens the door for her and pretends to bow. Cheesy! She spots us and calls over.

'Ready for the audition today, you two?'

'You bet,' I say with enthusiasm. 'Can't wait.'

'Good,' she says. 'Should be a strong line-up, but I'm sure there'll be a part for you both.'

She smiles at Muggs. I can feel him grinning at her. All the boys fancy her rotten, and half the staff, probably. It's funny, because she's not conventionally gorgeous, but she's got this waterfall of long curly red hair cascading down her back and she's little and bubbly with freckles on her face and arms and amazing green eyes. She's got a pair of boots exactly the same shade. She has a way of making you feel really special, like you could do anything you wanted. No wonder loads of people want a part in the play.

Trouble is, being Shakespeare, there are lots of parts for the boys and not so many for the girls – six to be precise, if Miss decides to include the Hecate scene. And there's no way I intend to be a witch or the one-scene, no-hoper, Lady Macduff. No, there's only one part I want and that's the lead; it's Lady Macbeth for me or nothing.

'I'd better warn you, *Macbeth* is known as "The Unlucky Play", you know,' Miss Taylor says.

'Why?' asks Muggs.

'Apparently it has a curse on it. It's supposed to bring bad luck to people who act in it.'

'No way,' scoffs Muggs.

'Is that true?' I ask, fascinated.

'Well, it's theatrical legend,' Miss Taylor replies. 'Why, you're not superstitious, are you?'

'I don't know,' I lie. 'I've never really thought about it.'

'Don't worry, your dad will be around to look after

15

you. I've persuaded him to be stage manager,' Miss Taylor says to me.

'Are you?' I stare at him. I didn't know Dad was interested in drama.

'Well, yes, I thought I might, that is if you don't mind,' Dad says, looking a bit sheepish.

'Cool,' I say, turning away as the bell goes. This could work to my advantage. If Dad wants to help, he'll have to persuade Mum it's okay for me to be in the play. I'm surprised, though.

'What's all that about?' I say to Muggs as we walk into school.

'He's smitten,' he says and laughs. I look at him, puzzled, and he says, 'He probably fancies her, idiot,' and then I laugh too. My dad? I don't think so somehow.

The morning flies by and there's only one thing on my mind. The auditions are at lunchtime and Miss Taylor has promised to put us out of our misery by the end of the day. The cast list will go up in the drama room after school.

I eat my lunch at break time and Ali and I go over our speeches together. Ali's watched the Polanski film on video and wants to play the scene where the beautiful Lady Macbeth captivates poor old, unsuspecting Duncan. She doesn't have a clue what's going on and reads Shakespeare as if it's a foreign language, but she certainly knows how to give Duncan the come-on.

I've chosen the really sexy speech where she's alone and she calls on evil spirits to fill her up with direst cruelty.

'How can you say this in front of other people?' squeaks Ali.

> *'Come to my woman's breasts*
> *and take my milk for gall.'*

'I'd die of embarrassment!'

'Oh grow up!' I mutter. To tell the truth, I am a bit nervous as to whether I can handle this speech, especially in front of Muggs and the others who'll be trying out. It's too late to worry now though, I've just got to give it my best shot.

And everything goes swimmingly. I'd studied it carefully last night and that article on the net has given me a new dimension into Lady M's character. I just think about Muggs playing my husband and about how I would do absolutely anything for him and go for it. At the end, everyone claps wildly and Miss Taylor looks really pleased. I knew I'd got it.

I didn't see Muggs doing his part but he's far and away better at acting than any other boy in the school. He's also totally dependable and if he says he's going to do something he'll make sure he does it, which Miss Taylor says is far more important than any talent he has. So I spend the whole afternoon in a dream of Muggs and me wrapped in each other's arms as we plan how to murder Duncan and, at last, four o'clock arrives.

Muggs and I go up to the drama room together, holding hands. I'm more confident than he is, I can tell, because he's so quiet, but I still feel sick. There's already a crowd of hopefuls at the board. Miss Taylor comes along with a piece of paper. She winks at me. It's going to be all right.

It is! There it is in black and white.

Macbeth . . . . David Morgan
Lady Macbeth . . . . Jessica Bayliss

Muggs picks me up and swings me round. I scream till he shuts me up with a kiss. Everyone congratulates us, even Ali who's green with envy.

Miss Taylor beams and says, 'Well done, you two. Rehearsals start tomorrow, four o'clock. Don't be late.'

I look again at the list.

'Oh wow, Ali, you've got a part! You're one of the witches!'

'Witch! Me! Puh-lease,' splutters Ali. Everyone laughs. Ali looks mortified. Miss Taylor jumps in to the rescue.

'Seriously, Ali. I want you to be the Third Witch. It's a most important part. The witches have to entice

Macbeth into doing what they want. Your powers of seduction came over well in the audition. I think you, Kelly and Jade will make a great team.'

Ali looks brighter. Kelly and Jade are two girls in Year 10. They also tried out for Lady Macbeth. I see where Miss is coming from: Girl Power. Those three will definitely give Macbeth a run for his money. Sounds like typecasting to me.

Dad comes up and gives me a hug.

'Congratulations,' he says, looking dead proud. 'I look forward to working with you.'

I find myself grinning from ear to ear. I am *so* lucky. I've got the best life in the world. Great parents, a fab boyfriend and the most amazing part in a play that anyone has ever had. Life couldn't be better.

Dad and I drive home together. I can't wait to tell Mum. I know she'll be over the moon, though she's bound to say, 'Don't neglect your work.'

I push open the door and yell, 'Mum!'

She's in the kitchen and she's crying her eyes out.

How can you eat a normal family dinner when your life isn't normal any more? We're all sitting around the table because Mum insists that we must eat, but pizza is sticking in my throat and I can't swallow. I end up regurgitating it like a mother bird and putting it on the side of my plate and no one says a thing.

Dad's pushing his salad around and poking it under the pizza and he keeps giving quick glances at Mum when he thinks she's not looking.

She looks the most normal of us all, now that she's dropped her bombshell and switched back into Mum mode. She won't let me answer the phone when it rings while we're at the table but she never does, so nothing new there. I can hear Ali. She leaves a message on the answerphone:

'Call me back, Lady Macbeth. I can't believe we've both got parts!'

This makes Mum sit up.

'Jess! I'm so sorry. You got the part?'

I nod miserably. It's not important any more.

'But that's wonderful! Well done, sweetheart. But promise me you won't neglect your work.'

I look at her and smile.

'I knew you'd say that.'

Then I burst into tears.

Mum's got breast cancer.

She's been to the Daybreak Centre today to get her results. It turns out it's the specialist breast cancer unit at St John's Hospital. She had a lump tested last week and hadn't said a word to anyone, not even Dad.

'I thought it would all be all right,' she keeps saying.

It wasn't. It was a tumour that has to be removed as soon as possible, which means that the day after tomorrow she has to go into St John's for an operation on her breast. It's known as a wide excision. She's also got to have lymph glands removed from under her arm to see if the cancer has got into her lymph system. Being Mum she's explained it all to us in detail.

She comes round the table and puts her arms round me. I feel like I did when I was a kid and would wake up with a nightmare and Mum would come and cuddle me. I put my head on her breast and then jump back.

'I'm sorry! Does that hurt?'

'Of course not,' she says and presses my face close to her again. I can smell her familiar smell, a mixture of cooking, Calvin Klein and a slight whiff of sweat. It makes me cry more and I hug her so tight it hurts. I don't know what I'd do without my mum.

'Will you die?' I whisper.

'What?' she asks. She considers the question. I wait, holding my breath, dreading the answer. Mum never lies.

'I certainly don't intend to,' she says finally.

'I bet Linda McCartney didn't intend to,' I say miserably.

'Jess!' Dad warns.

'No, it's okay,' says Mum. 'Do you think that thought hasn't occurred to me? No, as far as I know, the earlier you discover breast cancer, the better your chances of surviving it. They'll know more after the op, but Dr Hamez is hopeful that we've caught it early.'

'Will you have to have your breast removed?' I ask.

Mum looks stricken.

'God, I hope not. I'm only forty-four.'

Tears roll down her cheeks. Suddenly, forty-four doesn't sound ancient any more.

'That's enough questions, Jess. Everything'll be all right, you'll see. It'll all work out,' Dad says. He looks white.

He comes over and puts his arms round us both. We have a group hug.

'I wish Carly was here,' I say into Dad's shoulder.

'Don't you say anything to her when you e-mail her,' warns Mum. 'There's no need for her to know anything.'

'What?' I spring back in surprise. 'She'd want to know. She'll be mad if we don't tell her.'

'No,' says Mum firmly. 'I mean it, Jess. What's the point of upsetting her? She can't do anything. It'll all be over by the time she gets home. Oh and don't say anything to Gran either. She'll only fuss.'

I look at Dad and manage a grin. Nothing changes. Mum's calling all the shots as usual.

'Can I tell Ali?' I ask.

Mum grimaces.

'I suppose so. There's no point in keeping it secret for the sake of it. Those days are gone, thank goodness. But no dramatics, Jess. I'm not about to pop my socks. I'm just having a small op and hopefully that'll be the end of it.'

I love Mum when she's so down-to-earth. I feel better. I go upstairs to ring Ali. She's all excited about the play.

'I can't believe we've both got the parts we wanted.'

I grin into the phone. Ali has a unique way of rearranging life to suit her own version of events. She witters on about how romantic it is that Muggs and I are playing husband and wife and what a great couple we make.

'I'm so glad I've got the Third Witch and not Lady

Macbeth,' she burbles. 'I'd never remember all those lines.'

Too right. Because she'd never get round to learning them! But suddenly I feel scared that I won't manage it either. Then I think that if Muggs can, I can, as he's got ten times more to learn than I have. I wonder if I should tell Muggs about Mum. I guess I'm going to have to. Life seems to have become complicated. I sigh. I've got to tell someone.

'Look, I've got something I need to tell you. Can I come round?'

There's a silence at the other end of the phone. She knows this is serious.

'You're not pregnant, are you?'

'Ali!' As if! I've never even done it so I'd have a job on, but I wasn't going to go into that now. 'No, I'm not! Look, I'll be round in a minute, I'll explain then.'

I look in at Mum and Dad to tell them where I'm going. Mum says, 'Okay, don't be late,' and Dad just waves. They're sitting on the sofa, with their arms round each other, listening to Paul McCartney. He's singing:

> *'Will you still need me?*
> *Will you still feed me?*
> *When I'm sixty-four.'*

Normally this would make me cringe.

Today it makes me want to cry.

By the time I get home, Mum's in bed and Dad's on the phone. He puts it down when I come in.

'Who was that?' I ask.

'Oh, I was just ringing Cathy,' he says. Cathy is Miss Taylor. 'I thought I'd take a couple of days off. Be there for your mum. I've set work for my classes and she'll make sure they get it.'

Good old Dad. It's just like him to want to be with Mum and help her through this. I go to him and give him a kiss. He ruffles my hair in his Dad-like way.

'Are you okay?' he asks.

'Yep,' I say. Actually, I'm not. Ali's reaction has freaked me out.

'Breast cancer!' she said. 'Your mum's got breast cancer! Oh no, Jess, that's terrible.'

It turns out her gran died from it and, it sounds like,

half the rest of the female population that Ali has ever come into contact with.

Strangely enough, it's Debbie, Ali's mum, who comes to the rescue.

'She'll be fine, Jess,' she says. 'Give it a rest, Ali. Things have changed tremendously nowadays and your mum's as fit as a fiddle.'

I smile at her gratefully. I've never really rated Debbie much as a mum before. She's more like Ali's older sister. She never married Ali's dad and she seems to fall in and out of relationships nearly as often as Ali. She and Ali got their belly buttons pierced together. She's cool, but I'm secretly pleased I've got the boring middle-aged parents who've been married for ever and who spend their Friday evenings bingeing on a bottle of wine and a week's video-recording of *Coronation Street*.

And no, in case you're wondering, Mum won't let me get my belly button pierced. To be honest, I wouldn't want it; I think it's naff – or "passé", as Miss Taylor would say.

Anyway, I've had enough excitement for one day, that's for sure. 'I'm off to bed, Dad,' I say. He's sitting on the sofa and I put my arm round his neck. I kiss the spot where his hair is starting to thin, on the crown of his head. He pats my arm.

'Night, love,' he says. He smiles at me. He looks tired. Poor Dad.

Upstairs, Mum's fast asleep with the light on and her book open on the bed. I feel like getting in beside her like I used to do when I was little but I don't want to disturb her. Instead I turn the light off and give her a kiss on her forehead. She moves her head and mutters something I don't catch. She looks really peaceful.

Not like me. When I get into bed my head's reeling with everything. What a day! It's been the best of times and the worst of times. The witches' chant drums through my head:

'Fair is foul, and foul is fair . . .'

I lie there for what seems like hours going over everything. I replay again and again the buzz of the audition, the applause at the end of my speech, the cheers and whistles when the list went up and the sensation of Muggs's lips on mine. It's one of the best moments of my life.

Then I remember Mum dropping her bombshell and it's one of the worst. No, it is the worst. Cancer! The word keeps echoing in my mind. Cancer. Cancer's what old people get if they've smoked all their lives. Other people get cancer, not us. People die of cancer.

Calm down. I tell myself, Cancer's a sign of the Zodiac. That's all. It can't hurt you.

But it's the crab. It gets its claws into you and won't let go.

I toss and turn. My bed is hot and uncomfortable and I need someone to talk to. I text Muggs.

'I can't sleep,' I complain.

Back comes the reply, as quick as a flash. 'Macbeth has murdered sleep.'

This morning I would have laughed at that. Now it spooks me out. What was it Miss Taylor said about *Macbeth* being the unlucky play? Tomorrow I'll look it up on the Internet. I'll look up about breast cancer too.

'Fair is foul, and foul is fair . . .'

I get up to go to the bathroom for a glass of water. I can hear Mum snoring gently. I can also hear Dad. He's talking to someone on the phone. It's two o'clock in the morning. The world's gone mad.

At last I fall into an uneasy sleep where I dream of Mum and Dad and Miss Taylor, Muggs and me and Ali, and we're all running one behind the other in a decreasing circle, and chasing us is a giant crab. The witches stand by, laughing, laughing . . . I can hear a drum . . .

I wake up to the sound of Ali beating the front door down. We've all overslept. Dad didn't put the alarm on because he's not going into school and neither is Mum. She has to go to the Daybreak Centre for some injection. That just leaves me.

I suppose I could have wangled the day off, but I don't want it. We're starting rehearsals of *Macbeth* today after school. I tell Ali to go on ahead but she insists on coming in to wait for me. When Mum walks into the kitchen I understand why. She stares at her and says in a deep, concerned voice, 'How *are* you, Mrs Bayliss?'

'Fine thanks, Alison,' says Mum, irritated, filling the kettle. She's never been that enamoured with Ali and today it's easy to see her solicitude gets on her nerves. 'Why shouldn't I be?'

'No reason,' says Ali, flushing. 'It's just that you don't look as if you're going to work today.'

'No,' says Mum, eyeing her as if she's something the cat dragged in. 'I'm not sure what time we'll be back tonight, Jess. Your dad's coming with me.'

'That's okay, I'll be late anyway. I've got rehearsals.'

'Of course,' says Mum, brightening. 'Best of luck, sweetheart. I'll be thinking of you.' She pours two mugs of tea for herself and Dad. 'Now, get a move on, don't be late.'

I walk up the road eating toast. I can hear Ali's brain ticking over beside me.

'She looks really good, your mum,' she says finally.

'Why shouldn't she?' I ask, a bit too quickly.

'Well, you know, with her being so . . . you know.'

'No, I don't know. What?'

'So . . . ill.'

'She's not ill, you daft bat, she's just got cancer.' The words sound mad even to me. We walk on in silence till we come to the school gates. I feel a bit mean. Ali is so easy to put down. 'Sorry I snapped,' I say finally.

'That's okay, I understand,' she says happily, giving my arm a squeeze. 'Don't worry, I know what you're going through. And I want you to know that I'm here for you.'

I stare at her in disbelief as she swings cheerfully into school. Ali Brown, woman with a mission, to 'Be There' for her sad friend and her dying mother. I could strangle her.

Muggs spots me and comes over.

'Did you get your beauty sleep in the end last night?' he asks.

'What do think?' I say, putting my arm through his.

'You look good enough to me,' he says, giving me my first kiss of the day, if you don't count Mum's. 'What did your Mum say about your part in the play?'

'Oh, she's dead pleased,' I answer. I really don't want to go into everything now. 'We'd better go in, the bell's about to go. I'll see you at break.'

In English Miss Taylor comes over and asks me how Mum is.

'Fine.' I can feel Ali turning round and smiling

sympathetically at me and Miss. I feel like ramming her sympathy down her throat.

'Tell your dad not to rush back to work,' Miss Taylor says. 'His place is with your mum.'

She makes me feel uncomfortable, as if it's all more serious than Mum made out. Dad knows he should be with Mum, he doesn't need to be told. I'm starting to feel claustrophobic, as if people are crowding in on me. Whatever happened to personal space?

I guess it's for this reason that I don't say anything about Mum to Muggs when I see him at break. He's still on a high at getting the part of Macbeth. He's surrounded by a coven.

Kelly Harris and Jade Bottrill, two of the most annoying girls in Year 10, have got the parts of the First and Second Witches. Miss Taylor is hooked on the idea of a kind of girl band, with the witches using their sexual attraction to trap Macbeth. It makes sense. I mean, why would Macca be impressed by old crones?

The trouble is, they're taking their roles into real life and they're all over him like the proverbial rash. Kelly's fancied Muggs for years so she can't believe her luck. When I walk into the common room they look at me as if I'm something nasty on the pavement that should be scooped up and placed in a dog bin. Muggs detaches himself from their clutches and puts his arm round me.

'What you doing lunchtime?'

'French. I didn't get a chance to do it last night.'

'Too busy celebrating, hey?'

'Something like that,' I say. I can see the two witches having a slagging-off session in the background and I'm pretty sure I'm the subject.

Let's face it, most of the Upper School girls don't like the boys bringing in their younger girlfriends to the common room. Too much competition. I wonder what they'll make of Ali being the third member of their coven?

Normally, being the target of other girls' snides doesn't worry me, but today it makes me feel uncomfortable. I know it sounds daft, but Mum's getting cancer has given my confidence a blow. But this is definitely not the time or the place to go into lengthy explanations about Mum.

The bell goes.

'I'll see you after school at rehearsal.' I give Muggs a peck on the cheek. I know the witches are watching because I hear Kelly and Jade cackle.

'Can't wait,' he grins. 'Where the place?'

'Upon the heath,' I cap as I go through the door.

'There to meet with Macbeth.' He blows me a kiss. I smile back at him. He makes me happy. Maybe everything will work out fine.

Kelly decides to chip in.

'Fair is foul and foul is fair,
Hover through the fog and filthy air.'

The two crones burst out laughing. I rush out, pretending I'm late for a lesson.

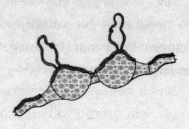

The first rehearsal is a general talk through. We're all excited but as soon as Miss Taylor enters, complete with clipboard, a hush falls. Some teachers have a real battle to get classes quiet but everyone wants to hear what she has to say.

She runs through the timescale. We're putting *Macbeth* on during the third week of September. It's the end of May now, so that means we've got four months to get it ready but, when you think we've got to take six weeks of the summer holiday out of that, it's not so long.

'So the first thing I want from you all is a firm commitment,' Miss Taylor spells out. 'If you can't give me that, you need to leave now. I can't have any of you letting the rest of the cast down.'

No one moves. Most people are veterans of school performances. They know what a laugh it is taking part. We had a ball last year in *Little Shop of Horrors*. It's this musical about a mad dentist with a man-eating plant. Muggs played the nice guy, Seymour, who saved the heroine (Kelly, yuck) from the carnivorous cactus. He was brilliant. I played the plant. It was baking inside the costume and I lost five pounds in weight.

'Good. I've written a schedule of rehearsals till the end of term. Obviously, some of you will need to attend more than others. You'll be glad to know that Mr Bayliss, Jessica's father, has agreed to help though he can't be with us today.'

Everyone swivels round to look at me. Much to my annoyance, I can feel myself blushing.

'So that's how she got the part,' whispers Kelly to Jade, loud enough to make sure I hear. My cheeks flame.

'Girls, girls, girls.' Muggs shakes his head reprovingly at them. Kelly looks embarrassed. Miss Taylor ignores it all.

'I'm going to start with the witches. I want to work out the relationship they have with Macbeth. The rest of you aren't needed today. Jess, look at Act 1, Scene 5, for tomorrow. Oh, you will be in tomorrow, won't you?'

'Of course.' Why wouldn't I be? It dawns on me that she's referring to Mum's operation. I feel wrong-footed, as if I hadn't been giving Mum enough thought. Anyhow, how come she knows so much about my personal life? Muggs looks puzzled.

'What's going on?'

'I'll explain later,' I say, as I edge past him. 'Come round after rehearsal?'

'Come on, Muggs,' calls Ali. 'We want to get started.'

The last thing I see is Kelly grabbing him by the hand and dragging him into their coven.

I walk home, my head buzzing, and let myself into the house. What a difference a day makes. Mum and Dad must be still at the hospital. The house feels different, empty. Normally this would make me pleased but today it feels soulless as if it's been empty a long time. I make myself a cup of tea and go on the Internet.

Miss is right. *Macbeth* is an unlucky play. All sorts of things happen to people who act in it: they have accidents or die; once even a whole theatre collapsed when the play was being performed.

I guess any play that's full of ghosts, murder, witchcraft and the supernatural in every shape or form is bound to carry with it what would nowadays be described as a bad aura. It's only natural. Or supernatural! Anyway, I'm not superstitious . . . am I?

'Step on a crack, you'll break your back . . .'

Don't be daft, that's just childish nonsense.

There's masses on breast cancer. Loads of it is statistics. One woman in nine gets it in the UK. How come I don't know anyone, then? Apart from my mum. More women

36

get it in the UK than anywhere else except the United States. Fewer women get it in Japan. I wonder why.

There's a lot about treatment too. It involves surgery, chemotherapy and radiotherapy in the main. It all sounds horrific. I move on to prognosis.

I wish I hadn't. Again there's lots of percentages and reference to 'five-year survival rates'. Is that all my mum's going to have? I read on and see that these are the lucky ones. My blood runs cold.

The doorbell rings and I jump a mile.

It's Muggs.

'What's up?' he asks, looking at my face. I pull him into the lounge and wrap my arms around him.

'My mum's got cancer,' I say, my voice muffled by his sweatshirt.

I can feel him stiffen all over.

'What sort?' he asks quietly.

'Breast.'

He squeezes me tightly. I can hear his heart beating softly.

'Shit!'

I feel the tears welling up and I start to sob.

'I'm so scared. I've been looking it up and it sounds really serious.'

'Let's have a look.' Muggs sits down at the computer and trawls through the stuff on the screen. After a while he says, 'Don't worry. It's not as bad as it looks. These scientific studies always give the worst-case scenarios.'

I feel myself start to relax and I sit on his lap. He kisses me and licks my tears.

'Mmm, salt.'

A key turns in the lock. We spring apart.

'Jess? Are you in?' calls Mum.

'Oh, hello, David,' says Dad, coming into the room. 'What are you up to?'

'Just a bit of homework,' replies Muggs, expertly clicking the mouse to close the screen. 'How are you both?'

'Fine, just fine,' says Mum, coming into the lounge carrying a pile of books. The top one has the title, *Managing Your Cancer.*

'I thought you'd been to the hospital,' I say, surprised.

'I have, but it didn't take all day. We've had lunch out, been shopping. Look, I got something for you.'

I open the bag and see the top I've been wanting for ages from Miss Selfridge.

'Thanks, Mum!'

'My pleasure. And now I'd better go and pack. We'll have takeaway tonight, shall we? And maybe a bottle of wine. Are you stopping for tea, David?' She looks flushed and happy as if she's going on holiday.

I'll never understand grown-ups. There's me, worried sick all day, and she's been having the time of her life.

In the morning she's not as bubbly. She's back to being Mum in a stress as if she's late for school and can't find her lesson notes or diary or car keys, which is a normal school morning. Nothing's right and Dad's getting it in the ear.

'Want some toast?' he asks. Mistake.

'Thanks, but no thanks,' she answers sharply.

He looks at her in surprise. She bites back.

'I'm having a general anaesthetic you know, in precisely five hours' time!'

'Sorry, love, I didn't think.' He looks crestfallen.

'No, well, you wouldn't, would you?' Mum is off on one. When she gets like this anything could come up. 'I wish I hadn't had those glasses of wine last night. You should've stopped me.'

Dad turns and raises his eyebrows helplessly at me. Dad could no more stop Mum from doing what she wanted than he could have stopped the tide coming in and destroying those sandbreaks he used to build on the beach for Carly and me when we were little.

'Didn't do you any harm,' he said gently. 'Helped to relax you.'

'Relax!' she sniffs. Then, 'Oh that reminds me. Where's my relaxation tape?' She dashes about in a frenzy of searching. Dad smiles at me wryly. I smile back.

'Best of luck. Ring me after school.'

Mum comes back in clutching a cassette triumphantly.

'Got it! You'd better get off, Jess, you'll be late. Give us a hug.'

I give her a massive bear hug. I must have grown because she feels smaller somehow, more fragile. It's a completely different experience from cuddling up to Muggs – all soft and squashy. We're about the same height now and our boobs press up against each other. For the first time it really occurs to me that Mum and I are both women.

'I love you,' I whisper into her neck. 'You'll be all right, won't you?'

'I'll be fine,' she says, giving me a final squeeze. 'See you tomorrow, good as new. Now, get a move on. You'll be late.'

She sees me out and I turn back to wave at the end of the street like I used to when I was a kid. Dad is standing behind her with his arm around her. They both raise their hands and wave to me. I can feel myself starting to cry. I see Ali waiting for me, brimming with sympathy, and I stop crying as quickly as I started.

The day flies by. Mum's having her op at two but I'm in the middle of a maths test then and it's not till I put my pen down I remember to look at the clock. I don't know how long it'll last, but Dad's staying with her till she wakes up. She should be home tomorrow, all being well.

Knowing Dad, he'll want to stay with her all night like he did with me when I had my tonsils out. He slept on a camp bed by the side of my bed and the other kids on the ward thought he was great. He raided the store cupboard and let them bandage him up like a mummy till the sister in charge found out and told him off.

'Coming down town?' asks Ali, trying to cram folders into her locker. She never does any homework.

'Can't. Rehearsal,' I say. I wander along to the hall where Miss is already waiting. It's just her and me tonight. She wants me to get to grips with Lady M's character and her first scene. When Muggs pops his head around the door she tells him to scram. He pretends to be hurt and I laugh.

'See you later,' I shout after him.

'What do you really think of him?' she asks.

'Muggs?' I ask, startled.

'If you like. I was actually thinking of Macbeth.'

I've thought about this.

'I'm totally besotted with him,' I say. 'I love him more than words can say.'

'Good. What sort of person is he?'

'A really nice bloke. Good at everything. Everyone likes him.' I could be talking about Muggs. This is going to be easier than I thought.

'What would you do for him?'

'Anything.'

'Anything?'

I feel a bit uncomfortable. Miss looks so intense and I keep thinking about Muggs.

'Yep.'

'Excellent. Never lose sight of that deep passion when you're playing her and let it motivate everything you say and do. Now let's hear your first speech, when you receive his letter.'

Miss Taylor is so good at drawing the best out of you. The teacher we had before her used to tell us what to do but she gets us to understand the characters and then leaves it to us. It's going to be good. *I'm* going to be good.

Time flies. It's easy, much easier than I thought, and I feel a real rapport with Lady Macbeth who's head over heels in love with her bloke and who probably wasn't that much older than I am now. You have to admire her bottle. She's prepared to go to any lengths to get what she wants for Macbeth and I love the words she uses to wind herself up to murder.

'Look like th'innocent flower,
But be the serpent under it.'

Huh! I knew a few people that advice could apply to, Kelly Harris for one! I'll ask Mum to go over those lines with me when I get home, to get them just right.

Mum. I'd forgotten about her. I can't believe I can just switch off like that. She's had a cancer op today. I'm a selfish cow. Miss Taylor sees my face and calls it a day.

On the way home my mobile rings. It's Dad.

'All went well. She's come around and I'm just going to stay with her for a while. Be home later.'

I let myself into the empty house. This is becoming a habit. A few nights ago this is all I wanted. Now I'd give anything to hear Mum clattering around in the kitchen. It's too quiet.

I go round to Muggs's place. It's definitely not quiet. Actually, it's mad. We eat junk food and watch trash TV in between wiping little noses and bums and chasing kids back to bed because Muggs's mum and stepdad have taken the opportunity of free babysitters to go to the pub. So much for a romantic night in!

I feel better though, cuddled up to Muggs watching some unlucky wannabe being evicted from the *Big Brother* house. Mum's okay and tomorrow's Saturday and we'll be back to normal again. I decide I like normal.

I walk home on my own as Dee and Ron (that's what they tell me to call them!) are still at the pub and I'm knackered. The house is in darkness. I bet Dad doesn't want to leave Mum. I run a bath and decide to go to bed. I'm asleep when Dad comes in but wake up when he puts his head round the door.

'What time is it?' I mumble.

'Not late. I waited till your mum went off to sleep. She's fine. Go back to sleep now.'

He gives me a kiss. I can smell alcohol. When I look at my radio alarm it says 1.45am.

It turns out to be a strange weekend. For a start, Mum doesn't come home on Saturday after all. I go along with Dad to pick her up at lunchtime and she's still sitting in bed in her nightie looking really fed up. There's something wrong with her drains.

'Sounds like a problem for Dial-a-Rod to me,' says Dad, trying to lighten the tone, but she's not laughing. She's got two long lines coming out of her, one from her breast and the other from her armpit. They empty a yellow sort of fluid out into two see-through bags and they look disgusting. Apparently she can't go home until they've finished emptying.

'Why is one coming from under your arm?' I ask.

'They removed a sample of lymph glands at the same time as they took out the tumour,' explains Mum.

'Why?'

'To see if the cancer has spread.'

She sees my face.

'Oh, don't look like that, Jess, it's only a precaution.'

It hasn't occurred to me that the cancer might have spread. I thought cutting out the tumour would be the end of it. I store it in my mind to worry about later.

'You look tired, Jess. What time did you go to bed last night?'

'Don't know. About eleven-thirty I think.'

'Too late,' she sniffs. 'I told you when you left, Rob, to make sure she had an early night.'

I look at Dad puzzled. I'm just about to say fat chance of passing on that message when he doesn't get home till the early hours of the morning then I notice him frowning at me and he gives his head a tiny shake. What's all that about?

Mum's going on about how I need my sleep, blah, blah, then the nurse comes to check her drains and I forget about it until visiting time's over and we're on our way home in the car.

'Do you want dropping off somewhere, Jess?' he says.

'Aren't we going home?' I ask in surprise.

'I thought I'd go into school and work on the timetable. Might as well get on with it while your mum's not around.'

'On a Saturday?' That's not like Dad. He usually mooches round the house and tries to watch sport on the telly while Mum finds him things to fix. Now he's got a chance to watch the footie in peace, he's going into work. That's men for you!

Mind you, he's got a point. It's not the same if Mum's not there. I feel miserable. To lighten the mood I say, 'School, hey? Yeah, yeah. Bet you've really got a hot date.'

This is a standard routine between us and I expect him to give me a description of the busty blonde he's going to meet, but he doesn't answer. I warm to my theme.

'And, come to think of it, where were you last night, Mr Bayliss? What did you get up to after you left the hospital?'

To my surprise he launches into a long complicated story about needing a drink, then having to pick up work from Cathy on his way home.

'Cathy? Miss Taylor?'

'Yes, she told me you were really good at rehearsal.'

'Not that good,' I say, taken aback. It's not like Miss Taylor to give praise until you've really earned it. 'I've hardly started. I'm not into the part yet.'

'Oh well, she's very pleased anyway,' he says, looking uncomfortable. 'By the way, best not to mention to your mum I didn't come straight home. She'll give me stick for not looking after you properly.'

I smile to myself. His secret's safe with me. I'm not going to tell her that he stopped off for a drink instead of rushing home to tend his precious daughter. I've been pleading for a bit more independence ever since Carly left and I became the sole focus of my devoted parents' attention.

He drops me off at Ali's. Debbie, Ali's mum, is coming out of the front gate with Ali's little sister, Lola, in a buggy. She stops to ask Dad about Mum.

'Give her my love,' she says. 'Tell her I'll call round to see her next week.'

That'll go down well with Mum. Not. Mum's never had a lot of time for Debbie and I don't think the sight of her in her tight skirt, high heels and low-cut top will be too welcome at the moment. Dad smiles though as if Mum will be chuffed to bits to see her.

Ali's in her bedroom playing her new CD and painting her toenails ready for a date with Sean tonight. She's all excited.

'He's taking me to the Star Bar,' she says. She's got a face pack on, so she's speaking through clenched teeth. 'I've been dying to go there for ages.'

'They won't let you in. You've got to be eighteen.'

'You wait,' she grins. 'Oh no, my face is cracking! I'll look sensational by the time I'm finished! Look what I'm wearing!'

She's bought a bright pink backless top and a tiny black miniskirt. My mum would have a fit if she saw me in an outfit like that. Actually, I wouldn't wear anything so skimpy. Mum's right, I'm afraid, I need more support. And I'm a bit more subtle than Ali.

'You'll drive him mad in that get-up,' I smile.

'I hope so. I really fancy him, you know. I think he might be the one.'

'Ali! Since when? You weren't that keen last week,' I protest. I can never keep up with Ali's relationships.

'That was last week. I've got to know him better since – a lot better,' she adds meaningfully.

'What? Ali, you haven't . . .!'

'Not yet,' she says, wiping the face pack off with big wads of cotton wool. 'But it's only a matter of time.'

'Be careful,' I warn her. I can see Ali ending up like her mum, with a baby in her teens.

'All right, Mum.' Ali chucks the cotton wool in the bin and opens her top drawer. 'I'm not daft. I was in the Brownies, you know.' She takes a box of luminous condoms out of the drawer and shoves them in her handbag. 'Be prepared.'

I must have looked a bit shocked because she goes on the attack.

'Don't look like that, Jess. You look like your mother.'

This really bugs me for some reason. I mean, why is

she having a go at my mum when she's not here to defend herself? Anyway, it's my job to diss Mum, not anyone else's. So I get a bit shirty.

'Well, I just think you're making yourself too available, a bit too soon, that's all.'

Ali goes red. 'What you really mean is, just because you and lover boy haven't actually done anything yet, you don't think anyone else should do it either. Well, I've got news for you, not everyone's frigid!'

'I'm not frigid!'

'No? Just as well. He won't wait for you for ever you know. Half the girls in school fancy him and they're not all locked up in chastity belts!'

I'm stung to the core. It's not like Ali to have a go at me.

'He's not like that.'

'They're all like that!'

I try to explain.

'No, Ali. We're really keen on each other. I mean, it's not about sex. I like him as well as fancy him and he feels the same about me. There's no rush . . .'

She turns away. I think she's not listening so I shut up. Sod her. Who does she think she is? Then I see her face in the mirror. She's trying not to cry.

'Ali?'

She turns round and falls into my arms.

'I'm sorry! I'm so horrible. I didn't mean to have a go at you. I'm probably just jealous. You and Muggs are really good together. Ignore me.'

It's impossible to stay mad with Ali. I give her a hug.

'Well, maybe you and Sean will be good together too. Just don't rush it, hey? Oh my God, I *sound* like my mum now!'

We both giggle then Ali says, 'I *am* sorry about your mum, you know.'

'I know. She'll be all right, don't worry.'

I wish I felt as confident as I sounded. I change the subject.

'By the way, you'll see Muggs at the Star Bar tonight. He's got a new job, collecting glasses. So you behave yourself, madam, or I'll hear all about it.'

'No chance,' she grins. 'I'm rocking tonight.'

'Have fun.' I wish I were going.

Instead I go home to an empty house – again! It's so quiet. I never realised Mum made so much noise before, or filled so much space. I text Muggs. He texts me back and says he'll come round after work. Oops. Dad might not be too keen on that plan.

That still leaves a long evening to fill. I wonder what time Dad will be home and then have an idea to butter him up. I'll cook a meal for him. This is seriously un-Jess-like.

I become Mum on a Saturday night in. I ransack the

cupboards and come up with an edible-looking selection of tuna, dried pasta, a bottled sauce and loads of fresh peppers, onions and mushrooms. I'm not sure of quantities so I err on the side of generosity. I put beer in the fridge to cool and some white wine, and toss a mean green salad. I find some garlic bread in the freezer and shove it in the oven.

While the sauce is bubbling away I get out a white cloth and lay the table, best cutlery of course. Never let it be said that standards drop when Mum's not around. I pick some flowers from the garden and stick them in a vase in the middle of the table. This is fun.

While the pasta's boiling I check my e-mails. Nothing from Carly. It's weird to think she hasn't got a clue about Mum. I wish I was at Byron Bay having fun in the sun. Life's not fair, as Scar says to Simba in *The Lion King*, the best film ever.

A smell of burning toast gets up my nose. Bemused, I look at the toaster before it dawns on me it's the garlic bread. Burned to a cinder. I chuck it in the bin and turn down the gas under the pasta. It's sticking to the bottom of the pan. The sauce is looking a bit dried up too. Where the hell is Dad?

On cue, the phone rings.

'I'm going straight to the hospital to see your mum,' Dad says. 'I'll be home after.'

'What about tea?' I ask. 'I thought we could . . .'

'Just get yourself something, Jess. Or treat yourself to a McDonald's. I've already eaten. Don't wait up, I'll be home later.'

'Give her my love,' I say miserably.

The sauce is smoking. I empty out the pasta into a bowl. There's a mountain of it and it overlaps into the sink. I scrape the sauce from the bottom of the pan. It's got black bits in it. I pile it all in the bin.

I'm so pissed off with Dad, like someone who's been stood up. How weird is that? I'm a mixture of spurned lover and spoilt brat. Suddenly, after a lifetime of fussing around me, my parents have deserted me without so much as a by-your-leave.

So in very mature fashion, I help myself to one of Dad's beers out of the fridge and open it. I take a sip. Disgusting! Nevertheless, I close my eyes and tilt my head back and gulp it down. It tastes vile but a warm feeling spreads into my belly. I finish it and debate opening another but the taste is so horrible it doesn't seem worth it.

A lonely Saturday night yawns in front of me and I don't like it one little bit. The beer has made me feel sorry for myself. I need someone to talk to. I wish Carly were here. I go back on-line and e-mail Carly.

Get in touch quickly, there's something you should know.

Trouble is, I don't feel any better after this.

I'm full of nervous energy and there's nothing to do. I go upstairs and pick up the copy of *Macbeth* from my bedroom floor. How the hell did Lady M cope, stuck in that castle all day with no one to talk to? No wonder she went mad.

I run through her first scene, where she's reading Macbeth's letter and waiting for him to arrive. Guess I'm her twenty-first-century sister, reading my boyfriend's text and waiting for him. Things don't change much over the centuries, girls. I decide to learn my lines. I recite them parrot-fashion in my head then I stand in front of the full-length mirror and practise.

'Come, you spirits
That tend on mortal thoughts, unsex me here
And fill me from the crown to the toe topfull
Of direst cruelty.'

'Unsex me.' Those words are magic. I continue the speech. It's easy.

'Come to my woman's breasts
And take my milk for gall.'

That's what breasts are for, not just to hang jumpers

on. I slip my top off and my bra and stare at my breasts. The words take on a power of their own as I gaze unblinking at myself in the mirror.

Suddenly, the doorbell goes. I pull the new top Mum bought me over my head and go downstairs.

It's Muggs. He's run around to my house and he's all hot and panting. He's clutching a couple of bottles of Bacardi Breezers. He looks gorgeous.

'Thought you might need cheering up,' he grins.

'That was quick!'

'Had to respond to a damsel in distress. Darren came in early for me, he needs the money.'

Muggs needs the money too. He did that for me.

We open the breezers and drink straight from the bottle. Unlike the beer, it doesn't taste like alcohol, though it warms my stomach just the same.

'Come in the lounge,' I say. We sprawl on the sofa in the dark, sipping our drinks.

'Did Ali get into the club?'

Muggs laughs. 'Last thing I saw, she was all over Sean on the dance floor. He can't believe his luck.'

'D'you fancy her?' I ask curiously.

'I fancy you,' he says and kisses me.

I'm in heaven. No I'm not, I'm on a paradise island, lying on the sand, beneath the palm trees. Muggs and I are wrapped in each other's arms. The sun is dipping slowly into the sparkling blue sea and there is no one else around. My skin is hot and smells of sun-cream. His lips taste of salt. The waves gently lap our toes.

Then suddenly, the tide comes in and drenches us in cold water. Or rather, the light snaps on and Dad walks in. We spring apart.

I'll never forget that look on his face. He's so taken aback he looks ridiculous, eyes and mouth wide open. No one knows what to say. Muggs splutters, 'Hello, Mr Bayliss. Sorry, Sir.' It would be comical if it wasn't so embarrassing. To my surprise I hear someone giggle. It's me.

Dad says, 'Just go, David.' He runs his hand through his hair and turns away. 'I'm going to have a bath. I want you to be gone by the time I come back down.'

As he goes through the door he looks back at me.

'How could you, Jess? Now of all times. What do you think your mum would say?'

I have no idea but I'm sure I'll soon find out.

I stay in bed in the morning. My head's throbbing and I've got a dry mouth. This must be what a hangover feels like. The phone rings and Dad gets up to answer it. I pray it's not Muggs. It must be Mum ringing from the hospital, because Dad goes out not long after and the next thing I hear is Mum's voice yelling, 'Jess! Where are you?'

I bound down the stairs and throw my arms round her. She looks fine; a bit pale, but otherwise the same as normal.

'Nice to be home,' she says. 'Now then, what have I missed?'

I look at Dad but he's fiddling with the video.

'Nothing,' he says. 'We didn't get up to much, did we, Jess? I put *Casualty* on to record for you.'

I breathe a sigh of relief. Good old Dad, he's not going to drop me in it.

'You angel,' she sighs, flopping down on the couch. I sit next to her and cuddle up. 'He's one in a million, your dad. Mind you, I've had enough of hospitals to last me a lifetime.' She puts her arm round me. 'What have you been up to? You look peaky. Late night?'

'Not really,' I say, trying to change the subject. 'D'you want a cup of tea, Mum?'

As I go to the kitchen to make it, Dad winks at me. It's our secret. Come to think of it, it's our second secret in two days, if you count Dad going AWOL on Friday night after he left the hospital. For some reason this makes me feel uncomfortable.

The phone goes all day. Word's got around why Mum was off school and all her colleagues are ringing up to find out how she is. She loves the attention and repeats the story of the lump and its removal ad infinitum. She gets a few visitors too, bearing gifts of flowers, and the house starts to take on the appearance of a funeral parlour. About teatime Mrs Shepherd, Dad's boss and my headteacher, turns up with a massive bouquet.

'Now, you take as much time off as you need, Rob,' she says. 'Make a fuss of Diane.'

'No need,' says Mum. 'I'm fine. I want to get back to work myself as soon as possible. We've got Ofsted in four weeks' time.'

'No, I'll be in school tomorrow,' says Dad. 'I need to get to grips with the timetable.'

'Guess what, Mum? He went into school yesterday afternoon and worked on it instead of watching the football,' I chip in.

'Did you? I was in all day yesterday and I didn't see you,' says Mrs Shepherd in surprise.

'Oh, I hid myself away.' Dad looks embarrassed. The doorbell rings and he goes to answer it. There's the sound of talking in the hall. Miss Taylor comes in with yet another bunch of flowers.

'Hi, Jess. Oh, hello, Mrs Shepherd. Diane, how are you?' She kisses Mum on the cheek and plonks herself down next to her in a flurry of flowers, perfume and smiles. She looks happy and full of life and Mum looks pale and tired in comparison.

I take the flowers and go off to make everyone coffee. We've run out of vases so I fill up some empty wine bottles from the recycling box with water and cram them in. I open a packet of chocolate digestives that Miss Taylor has brought and put them on a plate. She's thoughtful like that.

When I walk back into the lounge carrying the tray, Mum's deep in lengthy explanations to Miss Taylor about the operation and the consultant and when she has to go back for 'results'. Dad's watching them both and Mrs Shepherd is watching him. It's one of those freeze picture moments that we do in drama, a moment stopped in time. Weird.

Muggs rings me on my mobile because he can't get through on the house phone. I feel awkward and don't know what to say to him, so make the excuse I'm on tea-making duty, which I am, and I've got to go. It's quite late when everyone leaves and the phone finally stops ringing. Mum declares herself exhausted and takes herself off to bed. I'm not risking a one-to-one with Dad so I go up at the same time.

She's unpacking her bag from the hospital and I sit on the bed and watch her. When she slips her nightie on I get a glimpse of the bandages over her right breast and under her arm.

'Is it sore?'

'Not really. More uncomfortable.'

'I'm glad you're home.'

'Me too,' she smiles.

'It was weird without you.'

'Go on, I bet your dad spoiled you rotten.'

'I didn't really see that much of him,' I say.

'Didn't you?' She looks surprised. Dad comes into the bedroom then so I say goodnight and go to bed.

I lie there and go over last night's events and go hot with embarrassment. I wonder what Muggs will have to say tomorrow. Maybe we need Mum here to keep a lid on things, I think to myself. Well, everything should be back to normal now, is my last thought as I sink down into sleep.

Only that was *a foolish thought*, to quote good old Lady M. In the middle of the night I'm woken up by a strange noise. It sounds like muffled sobs coming from Mum's bedroom. I knock on the door and it stops abruptly.

'Mum? Are you okay?'

'I'm fine, Jess. Go back to bed.'

'Why are you crying?'

'I just had a nightmare. I'm all right. Go to sleep now.'

In the morning I've forgotten all about it till I see Dad coming out of Carly's bedroom in his pyjamas. The bed's rumpled. He's spent the night there.

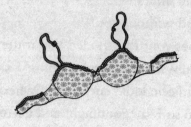

Dad seems fine at breakfast. He takes Mum a cup of tea in bed and asks if I want a lift. I say no.

To be honest, I'm freaked out. It may not sound like a big thing, but Mum and Dad always share a bed. I used to feel sorry for them when I was little because Carly and I had our own beds and they had to share one. Nevertheless, I would use any excuse to get in it with them: nightmares, tummy aches, earaches, you name it. The best bit was Christmas mornings when we'd open our stockings in their bed and I'd get to open Dad's presents as well. Oh, and birthdays, of course. It's the centre of our house, that bed.

I'm so upset, I tell Ali on our way to school that my dad slept in the spare room last night. I wish I hadn't.

'Well, it's kind of understandable,' she says, nodding her head wisely.

'What do you mean?'

'He's bound to feel differently about her, isn't he? I mean, that's a major op she's had on her boob. She's probably, you know . . .'

'No, I don't. What?'

'Disfigured. Perhaps he doesn't fancy her any more.'

'Don't be so stupid. That's my dad you're talking about. He's not that shallow.'

'He's a bloke, isn't he? I feel sorry for him. It must be really tough.'

'What about my mum? Don't you think it's tough on her?' Trust Ali to sympathise with Dad. Anyway, it's not about taking sides. I wish I hadn't said anything now. Especially when Ali goes and says to Muggs that I'm upset and tells him the reason why. Things are complicated enough between us after Saturday night as it is. But, amazingly, he's really understanding.

At break time he comes to find me in my classroom and gives me a big hug.

'Don't be daft, Jess, there's nothing wrong with your Mum and Dad. He probably slept in the spare room because he didn't want to roll over and accidentally hurt her in the middle of the night. When my nan had her varicose veins done, she wouldn't let my granddad in her bed for weeks. Mind you, he was a randy old goat.'

I giggle and snuggle up to him. He whispers in my ear.

'Like me. Has your dad forgiven me for Saturday night yet?'

I shrug my shoulders. 'I don't know. I think he's got other things on his mind.'

'We'll just have to choose a more private place next time.'

This worries me a bit. He's assuming there's going to be a next time. But then he sneaks a kiss and I hope there will be too.

Soon we are into rehearsals with a vengeance. Miss wants Muggs and me to get to grips with our parts, so we three meet every night.

'It all hinges on you two, you know. The play stands or falls with you.'

'No pressure there, then,' Muggs grins. We are discussing eleventh-century society with Miss Taylor, and the position of women. She makes us understand what she calls the contexts of the characters.

'Think about it, Jess. How does Lady M persuade her husband to kill Duncan?'

'I reckon she leads him on,' I say, considering. 'You know, she's a bit of a tease.'

'Exactly. She's got to use the age-old power at women's disposal – a bit of sexual persuasion. Call it love or lust: he'd do anything for her.'

'Women!' says my dad coming up behind us. 'They're all the same.'

He thinks he's being funny. Miss looks annoyed and Muggs looks a bit uneasy too. You see, Macca and his Lady get heavy pretty early on in the play and I've got to seduce Muggs in front of Dad. Embarrassing at the best of times; even more so when your dad has recently walked in on a real-life session.

To be fair, Dad doesn't take a lot of notice. He's got teams of kids that he's organising into sound and lighting crews. It's me who finds it awkward at first, till I start getting into the part. Soon, I've forgotten I'm Jessica Bayliss, virgin of Year 9, and I become Lady Macbeth, femme fatale of eleventh-century Scotland.

It goes well. I start to breathe, eat and sleep Lady M. She takes over me. Mum's dead interested now she's off work and recovering from her operation. It's good when I get home from school because she talks through the role with me and comes up with some good insights.

Then, Wednesday night, I get home from school and the house is like a grave.

I remember then that Dad left school at lunchtime to take Mum back to the Daybreak. I'd forgotten this was the day she got her 'results'. I wonder if she's as nervous as I get when my exam results come out?

Come to think of it, how long does it take to be told that your operation was a success? I glance at the clock and note in surprise that it's nearly seven o'clock. At that moment the front door opens and Mum and Dad come in. I can tell with one glance that it's not good news.

'What's up?'

Mum doesn't answer. She sits down and puts her head in her hands.

'Mum?' I'm frightened. Why doesn't someone say something?

'I've got to go back in.'

'What for?'

Mum doesn't answer. She looks awful. Dad looks worse.

'Have you got to have your boob off?'

Mum looks up. She sees my face.

'No! It's all right, Jess. Come here.'

She puts out her arms and I fall into them in relief.

'Thank goodness for that. I was so worried.'

It was true. But I hadn't realised it till that minute.

Then a thought occurs to me.

'So why do you have to go back in?'

Mum shifts and looks at me. She looks serious.

'Well, there's been some spread, Jess. It's got into the lymph glands. They're going to have to remove them.'

'But I thought you'd had those out already?'

'I did, but only a sample. Now they know there's cancer there they have to take them all out from under my arm.'

'And then will that be the end of it?'

'Not quite.' Mum looks uncomfortable. 'It looks as if I'm going to have chemotherapy and radiotherapy to make sure it's all gone.'

'Chemotherapy? Isn't that where . . .'

My voice tails off miserably.

'Your hair falls out? Yes. Only it might not completely, it might just thin. They're much better at controlling the effects of these drugs nowadays.'

I look at Mum's hair. It's dark brown and thick and glossy, like mine. She has it cut once a month and has blonde highlights put in to cover the light smattering of grey. It always looks immaculate. Along with her boobs, it's her best feature. I burst into tears.

'Come on, Jess,' says Dad, in his pull-yourself-together voice. 'It's just a bit of chemotherapy. It'll all be over in no time and your mum will be right as rain again.'

'Just a bit of . . .' Mum echoes. She looks at Dad as if she could kill him.

'It's not fair!' I wail. I feel about four years old again.

'No, you're right,' says Mum. 'It's not bloody fair.'

Poor Mum. She's spent a lifetime eating healthily and exercising properly and trying to make sure we all do the same and now look what's happened.

'Why you? You of all people?'

'I don't know. *They* don't know. I don't seem to come into the high risk factors. Could be a defective gene or something.'

I look at Mum aghast. I've done an introduction to genetics in science. If she's got that rogue gene, the chances are I've got it too. And Carly. Dad sees my face and leaps to the rescue.

'It's probably nothing of the sort. If it was as simple as that they could do something about it. Bad things happen, Jess. You think you can control events, but you can't, not totally. That's life, I'm afraid.'

Was I meant to find that comforting? Mum looks as appalled as I am.

Dad switches into action man and starts preparing dinner. Mum goes for a lie-down and I take out my copy of *Macbeth* to learn my lines for tomorrow. My heart's not in it. It occurs to me that ever since I got this part my life has started falling apart. Lady M and I have got a lot in common. Maybe we've both been cursed by evil spirits. I need someone to talk to.

I phone Ali. Big mistake. She's a total drama queen when I tell her Mum has to go back into hospital.

'Are you sure she doesn't need a mastectomy?' she keeps asking. Only she says, 'massectomy'. 'Because it's supposed to be much safer if you do have one.'

'Since when have you been an authority on breast

cancer?' I ask grimly. She's beginning to get on my nerves.

The weird thing is I can tell she's enjoying this in a strange sort of way. It's as if she's one up on me for the first time in her life. Her mum may have a succession of boyfriends and forgets to attend parents' evenings, but at least she's cancer-free. She's all concern and sympathy but it does my head in.

I put the phone down and it rings immediately. It's Muggs. He winds me up in a different way when I tell him the news. It must be a male way of dealing with 'women's things' because he's like Dad with an 'everything'll be all right in the morning' attitude.

'These cancer drugs are amazing nowadays,' he says. 'They've tailored them and they don't have the side-effects they had years ago. It's not such a big deal.'

No? Tell Mum that. Stupid blokes. Don't they realise how serious this is?

I've been on the Internet again. Lymph gland involvement is bad news. In a way, Ali's right. Crazy as it seems, if it had spread within the breast and she'd had a mastectomy, her chances would probably be better. Instead, Mum's cancer had sent busy little spores zapping off merrily into the lymph system, and even though the tumour was now completely excised, there was a chance those little spores could have seeded themselves elsewhere in the body. Hence the need for chemotherapy.

Shit.

I check my e-mails. Carly's answered my last message.

What's up? Are you pregnant? Worse still, is Mum pregnant?

I wish that's all it was. I type in my reply.

Mum's got cancer. She's having a second operation next week and then she has to have chemotherapy. I wish you were home.

How childish is that? What do I expect Carly to do? Kiss it better like she used to do to my cuts and bruises when I was little? Mum's right, I shouldn't worry her.

I press 'Send'.

I'm in trouble with Mum. You've guessed. She's mad at me for telling Carly. She's had a tearful phone call from my sister, who wants to come home to be with Mum.

'Why did you have to tell her, Jess? I told you not to.'

Mum's packing to go back into hospital and having a go at me is helping to take her mind off things. She'll be in for a week this time.

'She might as well finish her gap year, she'll only regret it.'

She puts in a new bra she's bought. It's seriously old woman. She gets defensive when she sees my face.

'I'm not wearing under-wired any more. I've read an article that says they can aggravate cancer. You shouldn't wear them either.'

'There's no way I'm wearing a contraption like that,' I say in horror. She's also bought a couple of really old-fashioned nighties that button up the front.

'It's easier for the drains,' she explains. Poor Mum. She's always been so trendy. Cancer is making her middle-aged.

'It's not as if she can do anything if she is here,' continues Mum, stuffing toiletries into her washbag. 'Aluminium-free.' She waves a deodorant in front of my nose. It smells vile. 'There's been a link between aluminium and breast cancer. Do you know, sixty per cent of breast lumps are in the top outside quadrant of the left breast.'

I look blank. She's really left me behind now.

'You use your right hand to put your deodorant on. You're more heavy-handed so more aluminium is delivered to your left armpit.'

'But yours is in your right breast – in the lower half,' I point out. She's not listening.

'You need to use an aluminium-free deodorant to be on the safe side,' she insists. 'And, by the way, there's also a strong link between diet and breast cancer. Do you know, hardly any women in Japan get it.'

Actually, I did know that from my Internet trawling, but I wasn't going to admit it to Mum. I'd be condemned to a lifetime diet of sushi.

'I'm going to read up about it while I'm in hospital. There's a lot of changes to be made around here, Jess.'

She plonks her pile of cancer books on top of her case

and zips it closed. My heart sinks. We're already the healthiest eaters of any family I know.

'Great, so now I have to burn my bra, have evil-smelling armpits and eat raw fish. I think I'd rather have cancer!'

Mum looks shocked and I wish I'd kept quiet. I don't mean it.

'Sorry, Mum. That was harsh.'

The trouble with Mum is, she'll make it her mission to find out everything about the causes and treatment of breast cancer. I've even had to fight her to get on the Internet now she's trawling the cancer sites. She's already joined the local support group and she's not even had her second operation yet. She'll probably end up fund-raising outside Tesco's and I'll die of embarrassment.

She stares at me and reaches out her hand to tuck my hair behind my ear.

'Are you all right, Jess?'

I want to say, 'No, of course I'm not, I don't want you to go into hospital. I want you to stay here and look after me, that's your job,' but she looks so worried I pretend I'm fine.

'Yep. But cancer's so . . . boring, isn't it?'

That wasn't what I meant to say. For a second she looks hurt but then she laughs.

'Dead right. That's exactly what it is. Now, you'll be all

right, you and your dad, won't you? And if Carly rings again, tell her to stay where she is and enjoy herself. There's no point in coming home.'

'Are you ready, Di?'

Dad's got another day off work to take her in to St John's. That means we'll have the geeky supply teacher for science again, who doesn't have a clue how to control us. Last time we had him we pulled a great stunt. Every time he turned his back to us to write on the board, we'd all inch our tables forward. By the time the lesson was over, we'd edged him into the corner and he couldn't get out. It was hilarious. Though, I have to say, it doesn't do much for our grades.

Mum gives me a big hug and grabs her bag.

'Behave!' she says. I wonder why. Has Dad been spilling the beans on me?

'See you tomorrow. Good luck!'

What a daft thing to say. But what are you supposed to say to someone who's facing her second cancer op in three weeks? She gives me a wry smile and off she goes.

I'm left alone and miserable. I wish everything were back to normal again. The phone rings. It's Gran.

We don't see a lot of Gran. Mum doesn't see eye to eye with her mother, as she puts it, on lots of issues. You'd never think they were related. Mum's super-organised and Gran, well she's different.

She still lives in London, where Mum was brought up, and she usually comes to see us once or twice a year. I think she's great but Mum's always tense when she's here so, to be honest, it's a relief when she's gone. They share one thing in common though: their gift of logic.

'Is your mum there, Jess?'

'No . . . she's . . .'

'In school. Good. I thought she would be. Why aren't you?'

'I'm just going, Gran.' Does she do this every day? Wait till she thinks no one's at home then ring for a chat?

'It's your mum I want to talk about. What's going on, Jess?'

'What do you mean?'

'She hasn't phoned me for the last fortnight. I'll say that for my daughter, she might not be a prolific caller, but she's regular. Every Sunday without fail, before she goes to badminton.'

I chuckle. Gran certainly knows her daughter. Mum calls it her duty call.

'She's also managed to have "been out" each time I've rung. Is anything wrong?'

Not a lot. Your only daughter's got cancer, that's all. I don't know what to say. I've already got it in the ear from Mum for telling Carly. She'll go mad if I spill the beans to Gran too.

On the other hand, it dawns on me that this is not going to go away. Mum's pretty sure she's going to have chemo after her op and Gran always comes down to stay with us in the summer. I make a decision.

'There is something you should know, Gran, but I think I should let Mum . . . or Dad tell you.'

There's a silence at the end of the phone. Then Gran speaks in a small voice, not like hers at all. She sounds old and frail.

'Oh Jess, they've split up, haven't they, after all this time?'

'No!' I splutter, shocked that Gran's jumped to this conclusion. 'Absolutely not! Gran! As if!'

The thought of my mum and dad splitting up is as unreal as Ali suddenly deciding to study nuclear physics. I laugh out loud.

Gran's reassured. 'Silly me. Forget I said that, won't you?' She's so relieved, she forgets to ask what the problem is if it's not divorce.

'Look, Gran, I'll have to go, I'll be late for school. I'll get Mum to ring you soon.'

I am late but I get away with it. The office staff let me sign in without putting me in the late book and when I walk into English, Miss just smiles and says, 'Sit down, Jess. I'm glad you're here. We're just getting to your part. Ali was going to have a bash at it, but you might as well take over.'

Ali looks a bit peeved but the others look relieved. She

would have struggled with some of the lines and there's nothing so excruciatingly boring as someone mangling Shakespeare. It dawns on me that I could get away with murder while Mum's going through her cancer treatment. I could be late every day, not bother to hand in homework, and I wouldn't get into trouble.

'Poor little Jess, she's finding it so hard to cope now her mother's got cancer. Go easy on her.'

Yuck. Anyway, I hate to admit it, but I don't think I could be late with an assignment if I tried. Like Mum, I'm too flipping organised. I immerse myself in my castle at Dunsinane and get down to Act 1, Scene 7.

It's this part of the play I go over with Muggs and Miss Taylor after school. It's a wonderful scene. Macbeth has an attack of conscience and decides not to kill the King. It's my job to get him back on task. I tell him he's lost his bottle and taunt him, using all my sexual powers to get my own way.

'What beast was't then
That made you break this enterprise to me?'

I'm furious he's changed his mind. As far as I'm concerned, it's an admission that he doesn't love me enough. If you love me, kill the King. It's as simple as that. Macbeth has let me down. I hurl abuse at him.

'When you durst do it, then you were a man.
And to be more than what you were, you would
Be so much more the man.'

That's the way to get him. Small willy syndrome. Men can't bear that, Ali says. Good old Lady M. She knows about men too.

The next lines I don't understand.

'Hey, Miss, I don't get this. It sounds as if she's had a baby.'

'So?'

'Then where is it? There's no mention of it anywhere else in the play.'

'That's one of the mysteries of Shakespeare. What happened to Lady Macbeth's baby? No one knows. Do you think it was Macbeth's?'

'What do you mean?'

'Well, maybe it was from an earlier alliance. Macbeth never refers to a son and heir. It certainly adds more interest to their relationship.'

So it does. So they were all at it in those days too. Nothing changes. Still doesn't explain what happened to it, though.

I turn my attention back to the words on the page before me. Can I say these to Muggs? I mean Macbeth.

The thing is, she pulls out all the stops here. She comes

on so strong that she says that she would have beaten her baby to a pulp while she was breastfeeding it rather than break her word to him. Bad enough. But it's the graphic detail she goes into that's the 'stumbling block'.

The lines are amazing. She spits at him,

> 'I have given suck and know
> How tender 'tis to love the babe that milks me:
> I would, while it was smiling in my face,
> Have plucked my nipple from his boneless gums
> And dashed the brains out, had I so sworn
> As you have done to this.'

And there lies the problem. You see, daft as it sounds, I'm embarrassed.

Muggs is waiting for me to go on but I can't. Miss notices my hesitation.

'That's enough for today. You two need to get together and go over this scene. That won't be hard, will it?'

She and Muggs smile at me. I grin back inanely. That's what they think.

While Mum's in hospital I thought I'd be really miserable, but the next day, Miss Taylor calls a meeting for the whole cast and springs a surprise on us. She's had an idea and it's the most brilliant, fantastic, out-of-this world idea anyone's ever had.

'I've been thinking,' she says. 'You're all getting into your parts and the play's progressing nicely. But what we need to make it really come together and be brilliant, not just good, is a bonding exercise.'

Ali rolls her eyes at me. We know all about bonding from PSS, Personal and Social Studies. We've been castaways on desert islands, entrepreneurs starting new businesses and survivors of nuclear war. We've seen it, done it, got the T-shirts.

'You're going to like this.' She laughs at the cynical looks on our faces. Her eyes are sparkling and she has a big grin from ear to ear.

'I've cleared it with the Head,' she continues, 'and as long as you get your parents' permission and we make sure all the risk assessment and insurance forms are filled in properly, it can go ahead.'

I perk up. This sounds interesting. We're all attention now.

'Come on, Miss,' says Muggs. 'Spill the beans.'

She strikes a pose and reads from the wad of forms she has in her hands.

> 'Time . . . Last week of August.
> Place . . . A clifftop in Cornwall
> Venue . . . The Big Rock Music Festival . . .'

She doesn't get any further. There's no need. We all jump up and yell at the tops of our voices. Ali flings her arms around my neck then does the same to Muggs. He's standing there shouting, 'Yes! Yes! Yes!' Kelly comes over to hug him but he grabs me and squeezes me so tight I can't breathe.

Miss stands there laughing at us for a while, then when we've all calmed down a bit, she starts laying down the law.

'The purpose of the trip is to really get to know each other,' she explains. 'By the time we get back to school, this play will be buzzing. We just don't have the time or energy for that level of commitment during term-time. Oh, and we get to hear some good music at the same time!'

Another cheer goes up but she hushes us.

'I want to spell out a few ground rules. There's not many but they must be adhered to.'

We're all listening.

1. Separate tents for boys and girls.
2. No alcohol, tobacco or illegal substances.
3. Everyone must be word-perfect before they go.
4. All up at eight every morning for four-hour rehearsals before the bands start.

Fair enough. A token groan goes around but when Ali protests, 'I'll never get up in time,' she's shouted down. We can't believe our luck.

The Big Rock Music Festival! I've been dying to go to a festival ever since Carly went to Glastonbury last year, but Mum and Dad say I'm too young. But they can't refuse this, it's a school trip – and Big Rock is *the* place to be in summer. Miss Taylor is a star!

'Three cheers for Miss Taylor!' yells Muggs. 'Hip hip . . .'

'Hooray!'

We raise the roof. As we all disperse, clutching our forms, Dad pops his head in to find out what all the noise is about. He's been building a set for Dunsinane Castle with his little team of Year 8 lads. He grins at Miss.

'I take it that met with their approval?'

'Did you know about this?' I ask him.

'Yes, Cathy did mention it,' he grins.

'I can go, can't I, Dad?' Nothing will stop me, that's for sure.

'Well, you'll have to ask your mum but I'm sure she'll say yes. After all, I'll be coming along to keep tabs on you, all being well.'

'You can't!' It's one thing having to put up with my dad in school; it's another having him breathing down my neck at a rock festival. 'You're too old.'

Miss explodes laughing. Dad looks indignant.

'Don't you believe it. I was at Glastonbury before you were thought of, my girl!'

My point exactly.

'Anyway, Cathy will need a hand keeping an eye on you lot.'

I decide to quit while I'm ahead. Mum'll know where I'm coming from. She'll put a stop to Dad's antics!

'Coming to the hospital, Dad?'

'I'll be there in a minute, Jess. I just want to have a quick word with Cathy.'

'See you, Miss.' Miss Taylor has always been the best teacher in Medrose High in my book. Now she's been elevated to sainthood.

I hang about outside in the yard with Muggs and Ali while I wait for Dad. We're so excited, thinking about a week of fun in sunny Cornwall.

'Think of all those bands!' says Ali.

'And the play!' I add.

'Sun, sea and sex,' Muggs chips in.

'Wouldn't it be great if Sean came too. Do you think he'll be allowed?' asks Ali in excitement.

'He's not even in the play,' I protest.

'He can help, he can be an understudy or the prompt or something like that. I'm going to ask her.'

'Don't you think you'd better ask him first?' yells Muggs after her as she dashes back into school. 'What women ask men to do for love! Sean, a prompter!'

We both laugh at the thought of Sean trying to follow a script of *Macbeth*.

'Miss'll never let him come. She's no soft touch.'

'No, you're right,' says Muggs thoughtfully. 'Shame about the separate tents. Still, I'm sure we'll manage to get around that little problem.'

He treats me to one of those lopsided grins that I find totally irresistible. My insides melt.

'I've got to go,' says Ali, appearing from nowhere.

'That didn't take you long. I take it she said no?' I ask. Ali avoids my eyes.

'I didn't ask her.'

'Why not? Are you all right?' She doesn't look all right. She looks upset.

'I'm fine. I've just remembered, I'm supposed to be babysitting my little sister.'

She grabs her bag.

'Ali! Did you want to see me?' Miss Taylor calls from the door of the drama hall.

'No!' Ali sounds abrupt. Rude.

'Wait a minute, I want to speak to you.' Miss comes out into the yard, followed by Dad.

'Sorry, got to go,' says Ali and she's off, legging it as fast as she can out of the school gate. Muggs and I stare after her in surprise.

'What's all that about?' I ask Miss. She looks worried.

'I don't know. Did she say anything?'

'Only that she remembered she had to babysit.' I turn to Muggs. 'I thought her mum picked Lola up from the crèche on her way home from work?'

He shrugs his shoulders.

'Probably remembered some boyfriend,' says Dad. He sounds as if he's trying to be jovial. It's that tone of voice he's been using round Mum ever since she was diagnosed with cancer. It doesn't work on her either.

I stare at him. He looks away.

'Come on, Dad, we'll be late for visiting time. See you, Muggs. Bye, Miss.'

She smiles, a small, worried twist that doesn't reach her eyes.

'Bye, Jess. Keep learning those lines. See you tomorrow, Rob.'

She stands next to Muggs, watching us as we get in the car, then she gives a small wave and turns away. Something's upset her. I turn to Dad to ask if he knows what's up, but he's looking so glum I decide it can wait till later.

When we get to the hospital, we buy flowers and magazines in the shop and go up to the ward. I can't wait to tell Mum about Big Rock but she's still muzzy from the anaesthetic and feeling sick. I hate to see her like this. She's got thick padding under her arm and the disgusting drain bag is back. She smiles and tries to speak but her throat is dry and Dad pours her a glass of water and helps her sit up to drink it. He's so gentle with her.

I'm sweating. I wish I hadn't come. I know that makes me sound heartless, but I can't help it. I hate hospitals. I hate the way the wards are always too hot. I hate the disinfectant smell and the whiff of something worse that lingers beneath it. I hate the noises: the moans and farts and retches that you can hear behind the curtained-off cubicles. I hate the bedpans and the drips and the syringes and the old, sick people in the beds. And most of all I hate my lively, bossy, capable mum being stuck in here with them.

My head's throbbing and I feel sick. I need some fresh air.

'I'll wait outside,' I say. 'Give you two time to be together.' I kiss Mum on her forehead. It's warm and clammy.

Outside the air is cool and clear and I take big gulps. I need to talk to someone. Muggs will be at work by now so I phone Ali's mobile. She's not answering. Where the hell is she when I need her? I leave a message on her answerphone to call me back and ring Gran instead.

She might do Mum's head in, but I love my gran to bits. As soon as I hear her voice, I go to pieces. Within minutes I've sobbed out the whole story to her and, though she's shocked, of course, to hear that Mum's got cancer, she calms me down.

'It's a serious illness, Jess, but it's not a death-sentence nowadays. She's in the best possible hands and she's got you and your dad to support her.'

'I'm useless. I'm not like Dad, I can't stand the sight of her like this. I'd be a terrible nurse. What can *I* do?'

'Just be yourself. Get on with your life. Show her that

you can get on with your schoolwork without her breathing down your neck.'

I chuckle, despite myself. Gran knows her daughter so well.

'And make a success of this play you're doing. She'll be so proud of you.'

'Thanks, Gran.'

'Be brave, my darling.'

'I will.'

I snap my phone shut and make a resolution. I'll be strong like Lady Macbeth and *'Screw my courage to the sticking-place, And we'll not fail.'*

Dad comes out of the door and does that thing where he runs his fingers through his hair and rubs his eyes. He looks worn out. He takes his phone out of his pocket, but then spots me and waves and puts it away. I walk over to him and tuck my arm through his.

'I've told Gran,' I confess.

He shrugs and pats my arm gently. 'That's okay, she had to know sometime.' He never lets rip like Mum if I do something wrong. 'But I'd better ring her tonight and tell her to stay put. There's nothing she can do here.'

'We're going to get through this together, aren't we, Dad?'

For a split second he closes his eyes and my stomach

lurches. Then he rallies and says, 'Course we are. She's over the worst now. *"Lay on, Macduff!"* '

I giggle.

'*"And damned be him that first cries, "Hold Enough!"*' Well done, I'm impressed. Didn't know you could act.'

'Oh, I'm full of surprises,' he grins.

'Yeah, right.'

That's one thing he isn't, my old dad. But that's the way I like him. Safe and predictable.

I get on with learning my lines while Mum's in hospital. Might as well, there's nothing else to do. Muggs is busy doing coursework and Ali ... goodness knows what's up with Ali. She spends all her time with Sean and she's dead moody. She's even rude and offhand with the teachers.

Like, for instance, we were in English the other day and Miss Taylor set us an essay on the themes in *Macbeth*. She started helping us with an outline and she talked about deceit and reality and how you can't trust appearances. It was interesting. She pointed out how Macbeth and Lady Macbeth were perceived as Mr and Mrs Good Guys in Act One, while all the time they were plotting to kill poor old Duncan. I was making notes but I could see that Ali was messing about a few seats in front of me.

Ali was nattering away to dozy Colin Stevens next to

her, who hasn't got a brain cell in his head, and giggling. Funny thing was, I could see that Miss was turning a blind eye to it. Normally she wouldn't take any kind of stick. Anyway, she headlined her favourite topic of REFERRING CLOSELY TO THE TEXT on the board and started to write useful quotes underneath. It all went quiet as we copied them down.

'Look like the innocent flower,
But be the serpent under it.'

And

'There's no art to find the mind's construction
in the face.'

And

'False face must hide what the false heart doth know.'

That's when Ali started sniggering, loudly. Miss couldn't ignore it and she turned around to face Ali.

'Do you think you know all about this theme of how appearances can be deceptive, Alison?' She spoke in a cold, quiet voice, not to be messed with.

'Not as much as *you* do, obviously.' The insolent tone shocked us all. No one spoke to Miss Taylor like that. She was nice. Miss flushed, a deep painful red.

'Ali!' I protested. 'That's a bit uncalled for!'

She turned round and glared at me.

'Is it? Glad you think so.' She glowered at us all and suddenly got to her feet and left the room, leaving the whole class staring after her in surprise.

'Time of the month,' said Colin, but no one laughed.

'Shall I go after her?' I asked, but Miss shook her head.

'No, I'll sort it out later.' Now her colour had receded she looked whiter than ever and her freckles stood out. Poor thing, she didn't deserve that.

I rang Ali when I got home to find out what was bugging her but her mum said she hadn't come home yet. I left a message for her to call me back when she got in but she didn't. The next day she was off school and soon I had more important things on my mind than Ali Brown in a strop. You see, Mum's had her results and it's not good news.

She's still in hospital but the ward doesn't give me the creeps so much any more. There's been quite a turnover since Mum's been in and the patients at the moment are a younger bunch. When we go in the sun is filtering through the window on to Mum's many vases of flowers and she's listening to an Enya CD.

One glance at her face, though, and you can tell that something's wrong. Her nose is red and her eyes look sore, as if she's been crying a lot.

'The thing is, they found more lymph glands were affected. It's more serious than they first thought.'

My blood runs cold. She's not going to die, is she?

'How serious is it, Mum?' I blurt out. She puts her arm round me. I lay my head on her shoulder. The woman in the bed opposite has her baby on her bed. He tries to dive off but her husband grabs him in time. They all giggle like mad.

'Well, they can treat it, that's the main thing. I've seen the oncologist and he wants to start me on chemotherapy as soon as possible. Next week if I'm up to it.'

How did all this happen? My fit and healthy mum on chemo. She's the one who keeps us all well. I burst into tears. Dad holds us both tight and pats my back as if he's getting my wind up. He keeps saying, 'It'll be fine, it'll all be fine' but he sounds as if he's trying to convince himself.

He gives me his hanky and I scrub at my eyes. The baby across the ward is watching us and he chuckles and claps his hands when I blow my nose hard. We all laugh.

'That's Alfie. He's Gail's. She's in for the same as me.'

I look at her curiously. She's got long blonde hair, which the baby keeps grabbing. She looks too young to have cancer, more like Ali with that hair, than Mum. I wonder if she's still breastfeeding?

'Gail and I will be starting our chemo together,' says Mum. 'It'll be nice to have someone to compare notes with.'

I glance at Dad. He raises his eyebrows and gives me a wry smile. Mum's networking as usual. Gail senses we're talking about her and waves. Alfie waves too.

'She looks nice. I bet you two are dead pally,' I say, waving back.

'Bosom buddies,' Dad quips. Mum smacks him on the arm and we all groan.

On the way home in the car, Dad goes quiet again. As a conversation opener I say, 'Doesn't look as if Mum's going to make Ofsted, does it, Dad?'

'No, sweetheart, it doesn't,' he sighs. 'She'll have started on her chemo by then. It's a hell of a reason for missing an inspection. Not much of a summer holiday for her to look forward to either.'

'You'll have to take her for a holiday in a posh hotel when all this is over,' I suggest.

He pats my knee. 'You're a good kid, Jess.' He's silent for a moment as if he's lost in thought then he says, 'Looks as if I might have to knock this Big Rock festival on the head too. She's going to need me around.'

Brilliant! I've got my wish granted again. The coast is clear for me to have fun with my gorgeous boyfriend and best mate in Cornwall without Dad around.

Then I immediately feel guilty. The reason he can't come is because Mum's so ill. Why is it that when my wishes come true, I wish they hadn't? And I feel so bad I hear myself saying, 'I could stay and look after her,' in a small voice.

There's a funny sound. It's as if there's a train approaching through a tunnel. It starts with a distant rumble and builds up into a crescendo. It's one of Dad's belly laughs.

He roars for a bit then wipes his eyes. I'm offended.

'What's so funny?'

He splutters again. 'Sorry, Jess. But get real. I mean, you look after your mum, while I swan off to some pop festival with Muggs and Ali? I don't think so somehow.'

Put like that I can see what he means. I stick my tongue out at him and he pretends to cut it off. I grin. Good old Dad. I sit back in my seat and put my feet up on the dashboard. I'm fourteen years old but my dad can still make everything right in my world. Where was Lady Macbeth's dad when she needed him?

The summer holidays come rushing towards us but before that we have end of year exams. After all that's been going on in my life over the past few weeks, it's quite a relief to knuckle down to some swotting. Ali misses a lot of them, claiming she's got glandular fever, even though the blood test comes back negative.

'It's known as the kissing disease, you know,' she says, when I go round to see her. She's in the garden reading magazines.

'Seanitis, that's what I call it,' chuckles Debbie, pegging washing on the line, with Lola, Ali's little sister, wrapped round her legs.

Actually, Ali's subdued for her. Normally, she's in your face but today she's quiet and doesn't seem interested in all the gossip. I study her as she lies on the lounger in a tiny bikini, blonde hair scrunched up on top of her head, long slim body taking on a lovely golden hue. It's not fair, if I lie out in the sun all afternoon, I look like a lobster.

'I thought you were avoiding me, you haven't been round,' I say casually. To tell the truth, I'm a bit peeved. Ali's always been my shadow, which has got on my nerves over the years, but for weeks now she's not been to the house. In fact, not since the day she ran off so suddenly from school. So much for 'being there for me'!

'Have I done something?'

'No, not you,' she says, sitting up. 'I'm sorry, I've not been feeling well.'

'Too busy wrapped round Sean,' says Debbie, disentangling Lola from a wet sheet. 'I told her she was neglecting you, Jess.'

'What do you mean, "Not you"?' I ask. Ali's expression is hidden behind her sunglasses. 'Who's upset you, then?'

'No one. It's nothing. Change the record. How's your mum?'

I pull a face. 'Not so good. She's started on her chemo and it's knocking her for six. Dad told me he can't go to Big Rock now. He's going to stay home to look after her.'

Ali brightens up. 'Well, every cloud has a silver lining, after all. At least we'll have a laugh without your dad around.'

'Ali!' Debbie looks really angry. 'How selfish can you get! Jess's mum and dad are going through a really stressful time and all you can think about is yourself!'

Ali goes bright red and mumbles, 'Sorry, I didn't mean it like that.'

'It's okay.' After all, I can't pretend that thought hadn't occurred to me. But I'm surprised all the same at Ali's comment. She's always got on really well with my dad and loved being around him.

'I'd better get going,' I say. 'Coming round later? We could get a DVD?'

'Can't, Sean's coming over.' Ali looks as if she's going to cry. Debbie stares at her, as baffled as I am. What's going on?

At last we break up. The cast are on a high because we're going to the music festival together in August. Until then we're going to have a break from rehearsals and spend our time learning our lines to be word-perfect for Cornwall.

We've all got our forms in and paid our money. I haven't mentioned it to Mum yet because she's so preoccupied with the chemo, but Dad signed my form and paid the fee. He doesn't want the money back either. Muggs and Ali have got to pay back their parents from their jobs. Lucky for me, Mum wouldn't let Carly or me have a job till after GCSEs. Spoilt or what!

Chemo's horrible. Mum goes to the hospital on the first two Mondays of every month and has injections of these powerful poisons that (hopefully) kill any nasty cancer cells that may be lurking round her body. In the meantime, she takes another drug by mouth every day for a fortnight.

The trouble is the toxins kill all the good cells as well. So Mum feels like shit and it takes her the rest of the month to start feeling better. Then it starts all over again.

What makes it even worse, if that's not bad enough, is that Mum has to sit with this contraption on her head, like a jockey's helmet with a big tube coming out of it, for three hours. It's full of freezing water. The idea is, it freezes the hair follicles and prevents the toxins destroying the hair shaft. So you get to keep your hair.

At least, that's the theory. It doesn't seem to be working for Mum.

Two weeks after she'd started chemo, I'm having a shower when I hear a scream from Mum's bedroom. She's taken to lying in after Dad gets up because she's not sleeping well at night. She was always the one who used to be up first.

Dad rushes up the stairs.

'What's up?' I'm dripping water all over her bedroom rug.

'Look!'

Her pillow is covered in dark brown hairs.

Dad goes into make-it-all-right-mode.

'Don't worry. We all lose hair, about a hundred a day. It's normal.'

'This isn't bloody normal,' shrieks Mum. 'There's enough to make a wig here. Oh God.' She shrinks back on her pillows. 'I'll probably need one soon.'

She looks totally stricken. Dad puts his arms round her.

'It's okay, Di, I'm losing my hair too. We'll go bald together.'

Mum lets out an enormous wail and pushes Dad away.

She turns over and sobs hysterically into her pillow. Dad looks at a loss. I feel like crying.

'Go and put some clothes on, Jess,' he says, sitting down heavily on the bed. The front door bell goes so I go downstairs, wrapping my towel more securely round me. I can hear Mum sobbing away upstairs and I can see a girl's figure through the patterned glass panel of the front door. I bet it's Ali. I'll have to get rid of her. I don't want her to hear Mum like this.

I open the door. Standing there with a grin on her face as big as the backpack on her shoulders is Carly. I scream in delight and throw my arms round her. My towel drops on the floor and I stand there as bare-arsed as the day I was born, giving my prodigal sister the biggest hug of her life.

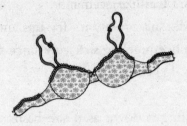

I can't believe I've got my sister back. She looks sooo different. She's as thin as a rake (I hate her!) and she's perfectly tanned – not that baked orange you get from a fortnight in Ibiza, but a lovely honey colour that makes her skin look as if it's glowing. She's got a nose stud and she's had her eyebrow pierced, but the most amazing thing is her hair – or lack of it! She's had her hair cropped so short it looks as if it's been shaved! It makes her eyes huge and she looks like a really pretty boy.

'I had it shaved in Thailand,' she explains, forking bacon and eggs into her mouth as she speaks, 'and when it started to grow back I decided to keep it short. It's much less bother. You should try it, Mum.'

'I just might do that.'

Mum has switched from being 'in a heap', as Gran would say, to being Mum again. She's cooked us all a huge fried breakfast even though,

a) she was bawling her head off in bed before Carly arrived and

b) she doesn't agree with fry-ups and

c) she's been feeling sick ever since she started chemo.

Carly's wolfing it down as if she hasn't eaten for the past ten months and Mum's grinning at her from ear to ear and parading round the kitchen in a sarong Carly's brought her back from Thailand.

I've got surf gear from Oz, T-shirts, trousers and a really cool wallet. Dad's got a didgeridoo. I pick it up and blow into it.

'No! Don't do that, Jess!' yells Carly.

'Why not?'

'The Aboriginals say that only men should play it. It's supposed to bring bad luck to women if they try. Something to do with fertility.'

'Great,' I say, putting it down quickly. Now I've been cursed by indigenous Australians as well as eleventh-century Scottish noblemen.

'How did you manage to carry it, Carl?' Dad's dead chuffed with it, blowing like mad into one end and going red in the face. 'Is there an evening class on how to play these things?' He manages to produce a scratchy wailing sound and looks pleased with himself.

'I hope not,' says Mum. 'Remember when Jess tried to learn the violin?'

'Nice one, Mum,' I protest as Carly and Dad groan. 'Let's all have a laugh at Jess's expense.' The house feels noisy and alive again. It's great to have Carly home.

We spend days catching up on all the news. She's had a whale of a time. Todd the Bod was left behind in New South Wales and since then she's been travelling with an American guy called Jake.

'Our next stop was going to be Vietnam, but when I got your e-mail I just wanted to be home with Mum,' she says, lying on my bed, flicking through my magazines. 'He's gone there on his own. He's a sophomore,' she drawls in an American accent. 'That's a second year student to you. He's *so* gorgeous.'

'D'you think you'll see him again?'

'I hope so. He's got a stopover in London on his round-the-world ticket so we'll try to get together then. And we're e-mailing. How're you and Muggs?'

'Okay.'

To be honest, I'm not sure. Since we broke up from school I haven't seen that much of him. He's been working in the Star Bar most nights and babysitting his brothers and sisters most days.

'When I see him he's always surrounded by screaming kids,' I complain.

Carly grins. 'You two need some summer romancing.'

'Yeah, well hopefully I'm going to get some.' I fill her in about Big Rock and tell her all about the play.

'What did Mum say when you told her about Big Rock?'

'Nothing. I haven't told her yet.'

'She'll never let you go. She wouldn't let me go to Glastonbury till I was eighteen. I asked her every year since I was fourteen.'

Actually, I'd kept meaning to ask Mum but she's been so sick the time was never right.

'It's okay, Dad's signed the forms.'

'Won't make any difference, Mum makes the rules in this house,' says Carly, flicking through my photo album. 'I love this one of you and Ali at Christmas.'

I look at the photo. We're grinning like mad into the camera with our arms wrapped round each other's necks. We've got the same stripy tops on.

'I was so mad with Ali when she bought that top,' I recall. 'I got it first.'

'Imitation's the sincerest form of flattery,' says Carly. 'She wants to be like you.'

'No way! She thinks I'm a swot.'

'Doesn't stop her copying your work though, does it? I think she's jealous of you.'

I look at her, surprised. 'D'you reckon? I mean, I know

I've got a few more brain cells than Ali, but I never thought that bothered her.'

'It's not just that though, is it? It's everything else as well.'

'Like what?'

'Well, you're better than her at drama, aren't you? I mean, you got Lady Macbeth, not her.'

'She's cool about that now. You know what Ali's like. She's forgotten she ever tried out for it.'

'Mmm. And there's fellas.'

'Now there you *are* wrong. Ali's got them buzzing round her like flies.'

'I know, but it's only because she tries so hard. She's a bit of a slapper.'

'Carly!' Talk about the pot calling the kettle black.

'I mean, it's not like you and Muggs, is it? You don't have to try hard to keep him interested, do you?'

I see what she's getting at. To tell the truth, I'm a bit worried about Ali. Since we broke up from school I've hardly seen her. She never comes round. When I ring she says she's seeing Sean or she's working in the café to pay her mum for the trip to Cornwall. It's not like Ali to shut me out. I wonder if she can't take Mum being ill.

Because, the truth is, it's not very pleasant. The chemo's taking a hold now and Mum's got lots of horrible side-effects. She gets mouth ulcers which make it hard for her to eat, plus she feels sick a lot of the time, so she's losing weight.

'It's like being pregnant again,' she groans, as she sits with her head in her hands one morning. 'Only I don't get a nice little baby at the end of it.'

She looks a sight. Her hair's coming out like mad and it's the dark hairs she's losing. What's left is like an old lady's, grey and thin, but she can't have it highlighted while she's on treatment. Her eyes are red-rimmed and sore-looking from the drugs and even her eyelashes are falling out, which makes her look peculiarly naked and vulnerable, not a bit like my mum.

I hate seeing her like this and I can tell that Dad does too. He's desperately trying to make things right for her but he can't and she gets fed up with him pussy footing around her. Only Carly seems to get it right. She's picked up how to massage in Thailand and she spends hours massaging Mum's face, shoulders and back, which helps her relax and feel better.

I'm jealous. All Dad and I seem to do nowadays is irritate her. And when I finally pluck up the courage to ask her if I can go to Big Rock, she goes utterly ballistic.

I pick my moment carefully. Carly's put the wind up me with her warning so I want to get it over with. I expect to have to do a bit of persuading but I'm sure it'll be okay. After all, it's all signed and paid for. I wait till Dad and Carly are out of the house and I've got Mum to myself. She's lying on the couch watching *Trisha* on TV, something that she would never have done BC (Before Cancer).

I wander over and plonk myself down beside her with a packet of oatmeal biscuits.

'When's Gran coming to stay?'

'Oh Lord, in a couple of weeks, don't remind me.'

'You'll get on like a house on fire now you're such a *Trisha* fan.'

She smacks me on the head with a rolled-up magazine and helps herself to one of my biscuits. We munch companionably.

'Do you want me to massage your feet?' I ask.

She giggles. 'Do you know how?'

'I can try.' She's got pretty feet, with pink varnish on her toenails. I wouldn't do this to most people, definitely not to Dad, but I don't mind Mum's feet. I get a basket of Carly's essential oils, a towel and a bowl and plump down beside her on a pile of cushions.

'Peppermint and Rosemary?'

'Sounds lovely. Not too much now.' Mum sits back comfortably and I pour a base oil into the bowl and add a few drops of each, like I've seen Carly do. Then I dip my hands into the bowl and rub them together. I take Mum's foot in my hands and massage it gently.

'How's that?'

'Heaven,' says Mum, almost purring with enjoyment. 'I didn't know you could do this, Jess.'

She settles back on the couch and I work on her feet. I'm enjoying it nearly as much as she is. She's all chilled out.

'You're a good girl, Jess,' Mum says drowsily. 'You're not having much of a summer, are you?'

'It's okay, Mum. It's not your fault.'

'It is. If it wasn't for this bloody cancer we could all have gone somewhere nice on holiday together.'

Here's my chance. I knead the ball of her foot and take a deep breath.

'Well, I've got the chance of a holiday. I can go away with the school.'

'Can you? Tell me more.'

I keep massaging while I explain about the trip. She listens while I talk about the play and the idea of going away as a bonding exercise. She wants to know who's organising it, who's going and for how long. Then comes the question I've been avoiding.

'So where does this bonding exercise take place?'

'Cornwall.'

'Cornwall! That's a long way to go. Why Cornwall?'

'It's the Big Rock Music Festival and it . . .'

She sits bolt upright.

'Oh, I'm sorry, Jess, that's out of the question.'

'What?'

'You can't honestly expect me to let you go to a Music Festival on your own. You're only fourteen.'

'I won't be on my own! I'll be with Ali . . . and Muggs . . . and loads of other people.'

'Exactly! It's a recipe for disaster. Oh come on, Jess, I wasn't born yesterday. I know what you'll get up to and so do you. I can't believe Cathy Taylor was daft enough to organise this. What is she thinking of?'

I'm still kneading her foot like mad as I say, 'Well, it's too late now, Dad's signed the form and paid, so I'm going.'

'Will you stop doing that!' She jerks her foot out of my grasp. 'He's done what? What has been going on in this household behind my back? I'm telling you now, Jess, you're not going and that's final.'

She's furious and she's made up her mind. Her eyes, red and sore, look as if they are about to pop out with rage. I hate her. The front door slams and Dad appears.

'What the hell is going on?' he asks in surprise. 'I can hear you outside. Jess, what have you been up to?'

I hate him too.

I don't get it, I really don't. I mean, *I'm* the one who's hard done by, *I'm* the one who's told she can go to a music festival and then is told she can't. *I'm* the one who's been there for Mum all the way through this bloody cancer trip, not Carly who just turns up to rub her back and becomes Number One Precious Daughter. *I'm* the stupid idiot who's been trying to keep this family together and who makes tea for my father who doesn't even bother to turn up for it because he's got something better to do. *I'm* the fool who never gets to see her boyfriend and whose best friend isn't talking to her. And *I'm* the cretin who gets it in the neck for sticking up for Miss Taylor.

The row rages into the night. When Mum says no she means it so I know I'm on a hiding to nothing, but I can't get over the injustice of it.

'You can't stop me. Dad signed the agreement form,' I maintain.

'You want a bet?' Mum glares at Dad. 'I can't believe you did that without consulting me.'

Dad looks contrite. 'I didn't want to bother you,' he says.

'Bother me! About my own child's welfare! It's a really stupid idea, Rob. All those teenagers together and a combination of music, alcohol and goodness knows what drugs.'

'There's not going to be any alcohol or drugs,' I protest. 'They're not allowed!'

'Not allowed! Do you think that'll make a difference? Honestly, Rob, how could you agree to this? Sun, sea and a raging brew of hormones. What the hell do you think they'll get up to? You should know better, you of all people!'

Dad looks embarrassed. What does she mean by that? I wish he'd stand up for himself.

'But everyone's going! The whole cast! I'll be letting everyone down.'

Mum stares at me sadly. 'I'm sorry, Jess, I can't possibly let you go. You're too young. I'd never forgive myself if something happened to you.'

'Dad! Tell her! It's not fair.'

'Tell me what?'

'Dad was going to go himself. Miss Taylor asked him to go and help supervise.'

'What?' Mum looks at him blankly. 'You can't be serious. Tell me, Rob, this isn't true.'

'No, of course I'm not going now,' says Dad, looking really shifty. 'Once I knew you were having chemo I told Cathy I'd have to pull out.'

'But you were obviously okay with this. Honestly, Rob, it's such a bad idea. What on earth is Cathy Taylor thinking of?'

'She's a brilliant teacher. She's full of great ideas! Come on, Dad, you were all for it!'

Dad rubs his hand through his hair but he doesn't say anything. Why doesn't he stand up for Miss Taylor even if he can't stand up for himself?

'She's bitten off more than she can chew with this daft trip. There'll be trouble, you wait and see. A whole crowd of hormonal teenagers! They'll be in and out of each other's tents all night.'

She makes it sound sleazy instead of the exciting, original, fun exercise it's meant to be.

'She hasn't got a smutty mind like you! We're going to practise the play, not have a flipping orgy!' I sound like a ten-year-old but I can't help it. I'm beside myself with anger.

'Everyone else is allowed to go. It's not fair!'

'Everyone else is older than you.'

'Ali's not. She's the same age as me. She's allowed!'

'Now why doesn't that surprise me?' Mum mutters sarcastically. 'Jess, this is my last word on it. You're not going. End of story. Now, I'm going to bed. I feel shattered.'

'But . . .'

'Leave it there, Jess,' warns Dad. 'Your mother's exhausted.'

Oh great. Now I'm to blame for Mum feeling ill. I don't know who I hate more, her for being such a mean cow or him for being such a spineless idiot.

Carly's nearly as bad when she comes in. I'm lying in bed with The Darkness belting full blast. If Mum can't sleep, tough. I can hear Carly downstairs talking to Dad. When she comes up she puts her head around the door and says, 'Bad luck, Jess. I told you so.' Very comforting.

I don't answer. I couldn't if I wanted to, I'm too choked up. I'm going to look so stupid in front of the rest of the cast. I can hear Kelly now, 'Little Jess's mummy won't let her come away with us . . . aah, diddums.'

And how the hell are they going to rehearse properly without their leading lady? I bang my pillow with frustration, wishing I were thumping Kelly, Mum, Dad, Carly and anyone else who has it in for me, and I toss and turn all night.

Muggs is gutted when he hears. He comes round

straight away. Mum's gone to see Gail, to compare notes on chemo presumably. Fun. Dad and Carly are out somewhere. We have the house to ourselves.

He sits on the foot of my bed and lets me rant on about the parents from hell, without a comment. Then he says, 'I won't go either. It won't be the same without you.'

I must admit, I'm pleased with his reaction.

'Don't be daft,' I say, magnanimously. 'What good will that do?' Then I add more truthfully, 'Anyway, it'll only give the witches more to bitch about.'

'Yeah, I was going to ask you about that. What's up with Ali?'

'Why?'

'She's hanging around with Kelly and Jade. I've seen them in the precinct together.'

'Bloody hell! My parents are screwing up my life, I've got no support from my sister and now my best mate's deserted me!' I'm genuinely hurt.

'At least you've got me to rely on.' Muggs pushes my hair behind my ear.

'Yeah.' I put my arms round his neck and he kisses me.

'You're beautiful,' he says and I smile. Thank goodness someone loves me. He kisses me again, a long slow kiss, and I sink into his arms.

I feel safe.

I feel wanted.

I feel his hand moving up my T-shirt to touch my breast.

The next minute he's on the floor looking surprised. I didn't know I could push him that hard.

'What's all that about?' he says, sitting up, rubbing his elbow where he's landed awkwardly.

'Don't . . .'

'I'm sorry. I thought you liked me.'

'I do.' I glance at him and look away. He looks flushed and I'm embarrassed. I wish he'd get up off the floor.

'It's my Mum.'

There's a moment of silence. Muggs looks dismayed. He scrambles to his feet. 'Oh Jess, I'm really sorry, I never thought . . .'

I stare at him blankly. What is he on about? Then it hits me — oh, God, he thinks I'm worried about Mum. Cancer. He thinks I'm scared I'll get cancer too if he touches my breasts. You can't get breast cancer from having your boobs squeezed, can you? It strikes me that's a question I can never ask Mum.

'It's not that.'

'What's the matter, then?' He's puzzled.

I feel awkward, stupid. I get off the bed and start brushing my hair with short, savage strokes.

'It's her. It's proving her right, isn't it? I mean, it's what she said, "All those raging hormones". Look at us, as soon as we're left on our own, we're at it.'

'No way,' he says. He looks upset. 'There's loads more to our relationship than a quick feel. If it was just that I'd have dumped you ages ago.'

'Thanks,' I say, stung to the quick. 'So I'm a bit of a disappointment in that line, am I?' I remember Ali's words, *He won't wait around for you for ever, you know.*

'Come off it, Jess. That's not what I said.'

Muggs is livid. I've never seen him angry before. I know he's right but I can't stop now I've started.

'You could've fooled me. Well, if it's sex you want I suggest you go looking for it elsewhere. I'm sure Kelly Harris will be happy to oblige!'

I don't know what's got into me. I know what I'm saying is rubbish but I can't stop myself. It's as if I'm possessed. Muggs glares at me for a minute then abruptly turns and makes for the door.

'Stop playing games, Jess. I'll call you later.'

The door slams. I'm left on my own. Alone.

You know something? There's a point in your life when you think that things couldn't possibly get any worse. How wrong can you be?

I'm really pissed off when Muggs walks out on me. At first I'm mad at him but then I start to feel guilty. To be honest I feel a bit of a tease, leading him on then putting the brakes on. And he'd been so sweet about it too. I wish I had Ali to talk to.

Then I get a text in the middle of the night.

It says, `Why do you keep alone`
`Of sorriest fancies your companions making?'`

I text back, `Hey! That's my line! By the way, I'm sorry.'`

Back comes the message, `No, I'm sorry. I should be more understanding.'`

I reply, `Yes, you bloody well should be!'

We've survived our first proper fight. He takes me out for a Chinese to make up – another first – and we talk and talk. From now on, we're going to be honest and open with each other about our feelings.

'It's not that I don't like you,' I explain. 'It's just that it's all going so fast and I feel as if we should slow things down a bit, at least till the exams and the play are over.'

'Course you do,' Muggs says, picking up my hand and turning it over to trace my love line with his finger. 'You've got enough on your plate at the moment, with your mum and that. And anyway . . .' He tails off.

'What?'

'Nothing.'

'Go on! No secrets, remember.'

'Well . . .' He does his lopsided grin. 'It's your brains I'm after, not your body. I don't fancy you a bit.'

'Pig!' I chuck the menu at him. He ducks and it catches the bloke on the table behind him and I have to apologise. Trust me!

He's so cut up about me not being allowed to go to Big Rock.

'I told Ali last night. She was in the Star Bar with Sean.'

'Huh! Bet she had a laugh when she heard I can't

118

go.' I sip the sparkling wine Muggs has ordered. After all, it's a celebration. Well, a milestone at least. I can't decide between prawns with cashew nuts or beef in black bean sauce. Life must be a lot simpler if you're vegetarian.

I'm still mad that she's been seen hanging round with Kelly and Jade.

'No, she was really upset for you. She said she was going to ring you.'

'Hmm.' Secretly I'm pleased. I've missed Ali more than I could have imagined. You get attached to your shadow. I giggle at the thought of Ali attached to my feet, a noisier version of me, and the bubbles go up my nose. I splutter and cough and the woman at the counter ordering a takeaway turns around. She's got long red curls, escaping from clasps on the top of her head. She waves.

'Look, it's Miss Taylor.'

Muggs turns round.

'Oh God, she's coming over. I'll have to tell her I can't go to Cornwall.'

'Hi, you two. What's the occasion?' She's wearing stripy leggings, her green boots and an orange furry jacket that clashes with her hair. I wouldn't be seen dead in them but she looks great.

'Um, it's a peace offering after our first row,' grins Muggs.

'The best bit of a relationship,' smiles Miss back at him. 'Making up after an argument.'

'Miss, I've got some bad news, I'm afraid,' I say.

'Oh, yes, I'm really sorry, Jess. You can't come on the trip, can you?'

'How do you know?' I stare at her curiously. She goes red.

'Your dad phoned me to let me know. Look, don't worry about it, we can manage without you. I know you'll be word-perfect and you have a real feel for your character. There are others I'm more concerned about, like the witches, to be honest . . . and the porter . . . and Lennox.'

She's wittering on as if she's embarrassed or been caught out doing something she shouldn't. It should be me who's embarrassed with a bottle of bubbly in front of me, more fodder for Mum, but she doesn't seem to notice.

'Actually, there's a possibility it might not go ahead at all.'

'What? Why not?' I can't believe what I'm hearing.

Miss looks uncomfortable. 'Well, now your dad isn't free to come with us, we'll need another member of staff.'

'So?'

She laughs ruefully. 'Unbelievable as it may be to you, not every teacher wants to give up a week of their summer holiday to accompany a coach load of teenagers to a music festival.'

'So it might not go ahead?' Poor Muggs, he's trying not to look gutted.

'Possibly. I'll have to see what magic I can perform.' Miss looks as crestfallen as Muggs. 'I'd better go. I think my meal's ready.'

As she walks out clutching her brown paper bag, she gives us a wave and calls over, 'How's your mum, Jess?'

'Not so good,' I say shortly. I still haven't forgiven Mum for Big Rock.

'Tell her I'll be around to see her soon. I've got some books for her.' She gives me a wink. I raise my eyebrows at Muggs and shake my head. Teachers!

A few days later I get a call from Ali.

'I'm really sorry you can't come to Cornwall,' she says. She's sincere. I can always tell.

'Why have you been avoiding me?' I ask, to the point as usual.

'I haven't . . . that is . . . I'm sorry . . . alright, I have,' she admits.

'Why?'

'Look, it's complicated . . . it's not you . . . it's nothing.'

I raise my eyes to Heaven. Dead right. It's something and nothing.

'Just come round,' I say. 'I've missed you.'

'When?'

'Now.'

There's a pause.

'Is your dad in?'

'What? No, just me and Mum. Why?'

'Nothing. I'm on my way.'

She is seriously weird. Five minutes later the doorbell rings and I hear her talking to Mum. Even Mum sounds thrilled to see her.

'Hello, Ali. We've missed you. How's things?'

'Great thanks, Mrs Bayliss. Mum sends her love. She'd like to come and see you but she says she'll ring first.'

'That'll be lovely, Ali. I'd like that.' Mum sounds genuinely pleased at the prospect of a visit from Debbie and her piercings. 'Go on upstairs. Jess is waiting for you.'

There's a pounding of feet on the stairs and Ali's face appears grinning round the door.

'Am I still welcome?'

'Is the Pope a Catholic?'

'Good. Because I've brought my brand-new waxing kit with me. We are going to tackle our facial hair problems.' She brandishes a blue plastic make-up box.

'What facial hair problem?'

'Upper lip, my dear. No woman is safe from the dreaded werewolf look.'

We collapse giggling on the bed. It's good to have Ali around again. Mum knocks on the door.

'Do you want coffee, you two? What are you up to?'

'Yes please, Mrs Bayliss. Just a little pedicure.'

'You haven't got anything in your box of tricks to make hair grow, have you?'

We stifle our giggles till Mum's gone back downstairs and then let rip.

'Not fair is it? We're trying to get rid of our hair and Mum's trying to hang on to hers.'

'Actually, I really admire your mum,' says Ali, recovering at last and taking out various tubes of cream.

'Hmm. You wouldn't say that if she'd stopped you from going on the best trip ever.'

'No, that's harsh,' agrees Ali. 'But you've got to hand it to her, she's coping with all her horrible treatment really well. My mum thinks she's amazing.'

I suppose she's got a point. We spend a brilliant afternoon getting to grips with our facial hair – literally. Actually, I reckon I do have a very slight down on my upper lip, probably as I'm quite dark.

'The Latino look, darling,' drawls Ali in a deep voice as she expertly pulls a waxing strip from under my nose. I scream.

I feel as if my skin has come off, but there's just a few tiny light-coloured hairs attached to the strip.

'My turn,' I say grimly. To be fair, Ali lets me have a go at her even though there's not a hair in sight. We contemplate doing our eyebrows but I've seen how Mum's have thinned on chemo and I don't like the bald look. So we paint our toenails instead in case Mum asks about our 'pedicure'.

Ali explains how she only met up with Kelly and Jade to practise the witches' scene.

'In the precinct?' I say sarcastically.

'There was nowhere else to go. We all live too far away from each other to meet at our houses. I don't like them, honest I don't, Jess. It's obvious Kelly just uses me to find out about you and Muggs. She's got a real thing about him. I wouldn't trust her as far as I'd throw her.'

'Yeah, well she's got no chance.' I'm feeling more secure than ever about Muggs since our row, not that he's ever given me any reason to think he'd play around. 'We're better than ever.'

'Lucky thing.' Ali looks a bit wistful.

'Why? How's Sean?'

'Oh, you know . . .' She shrugs her shoulders. 'It's my longest relationship yet. But it's not like you and Muggs.'

'Give it a chance,' I say, trying to stop the polish from dripping on my quilt. 'Chuck us that towel, Ali.'

Ali leans across to reach the towel and glances out of the window.

'Oh no, what's *she* doing here?' she says. She stands up and glares down at the street. I get up to look. Miss Taylor is coming along, green boots clicking on the pavement, carrying a pile of books.

'She said she was going to pop in and see Mum,' I answer.

'Blooming cheek,' mutters Ali with a scowl on her face.

'Ali! What's got into you? I thought you liked her.' I'm surprised at her reaction.

'Yeah, well, you thought wrong.' We can hear Mum answering the doorbell and ushering Miss Taylor into the kitchen. They chat for ages; you can hear their voices, a low murmur, rising and falling. I want to ask Ali why she doesn't like Miss any more but her face is all closed up and I know I won't get anything out of her.

Then Mum calls up, 'More coffee, you two?'

'Coming,' I yell back. 'Let's go down,' I say to Ali.

'No, I've got to go.' She packs her stuff up.

'By the way, have you heard the trip might be off?'

'No! Why?'

'Can't go without another teacher to supervise.'

'Oh well, I'm not bothered,' Ali remarks. 'It won't be the same without you anyway.'

Aah. It's nice to have Ali back on board.

By the time we get downstairs, Dad and Carly are home. They've been uni shopping for Carly and they've bought a duvet, a kettle, a toaster, a sandwich maker and loads of stationery. Carly's pulling everything out to show Mum.

I can't help feeling sorry for Mum. Normally she'd be darting round the shops with Carly, but she can't face the precinct. It's too busy and she's sick of people asking her how she is.

Ali's about to sneak off, but Mum calls her into the kitchen to inspect Carly's purchases.

'That'll be you next, Ali, off to university,' Dad says. He's too loud and he sounds false. It's a daft thing to say as well, because it's years before Ali's ready to apply to uni and she's never going to get there anyway, we all know that. Ali rolls her eyes at me.

He hands Miss Taylor a mug of coffee and she gives him a small smile. There's an awkward silence. Miss Taylor tries to fill it.

'Looking forward to going to Cornwall, Ali?' She sounds as if she's trying to court popularity.

'Not really,' says Ali. 'It won't be the same without Jess.'

Ali's so cool.

Mum has the grace to look upset. Miss looks as if she wishes the floor would swallow her up.

Then Ali asks, 'Why, is it still on? I thought you needed another member of staff?'

'We did,' says Miss eagerly. She seems anxious to

placate Ali. 'But Diane and I have been talking and she's agreed that Mr Bayliss should honour the arrangement that's been made in order that the trip should go ahead.'

'Does this mean that I get to go after all? Thanks, Mum!' I'm over the moon.

'No, Jess, of course not. That's a separate issue entirely.'

'What?' I can't believe my ears. 'Dad gets to go and I don't? You must be joking!' This can't be happening. I am beside myself with fury. I open my mouth to tell my mother what I think of her.

'YOU BITCH!'

Only it's not me. And it's not aimed at Mum.

It's Ali. And she's talking to Miss Taylor. Who looks white as a sheet.

Everyone's shocked. Even me, even though that's what I wanted to say to Mum. I mean, I'm pleased that Ali's standing up for me. But why is she having a go at Miss Taylor? The nicest teacher in the school. It's Mum's fault I can't go, not hers.

Only the weird thing is that Miss Taylor doesn't look annoyed at being called a bitch by Ali Brown. She looks . . . ashamed. And Ali isn't finished yet. She's beside herself with rage.

'You wangled that to suit yourself, didn't you? How could you? How could you both?'

She's looking at Dad as well. He rubs his hair as he always does when he's tired or upset, and avoids her eyes.

'I liked you, both of you! I respected you! How could you?'

'You've got it all wrong, Ali,' says Dad. He puts his hand on her arm but she shakes it off angrily.

'I saw you!' she screams. 'In the drama room. Remember?'

There's a choking sound. It's Miss. She's looking at Mum who's standing there, silent as the grave, little wisps of hair sticking out of her scalp. Carly moves over to Mum and puts her arm round her shoulders. She looks stunned.

'What's going on?' I ask.

'It's not what you think,' Dad says. 'Ali, you'd better go.'

'I don't *think* anything . . . I don't get it!' I shout. 'Tell me what's going on, Ali!'

Ali is silent now, tears pouring down her cheeks. And suddenly it dawns on me exactly why she's been avoiding me lately.

It all starts to fall into place. Dad, always hanging round Miss Taylor, offering to help with the play. The late night phone calls. The sudden fascination with the timetable. Dad going absent when Mum was in hospital.

'*Best not to mention it to your mum . . .*'

Our little secret. I won't tell on you if you don't tell on me. Wink, wink, nudge, nudge.

What was it he said when he caught Muggs and me going for it?

'*How could you, Jess? Now, of all times.*'

The hypocrite!

And Ali knew. That's why she's been so funny with me. That's why she wouldn't come to the house. I thought it was me she'd fallen out with.

I was wrong. It was my dad. Only it's too preposterous for words.

Dad's having an affair with Miss Taylor.

When I was little I believed two things about my parents. I thought:

1. My mum knew everything in the world.
2. My dad could put everything right in the world.

To tell the truth, pathetic as it may seem, I don't really think I'd changed my opinion about them as I got older. Only I'm wrong on both counts, aren't I?

Because Mum didn't have a clue what was going on and it's Dad who's made our world go wrong.

Is this what's known as growing up?

It's Carly who takes charge. Mum just looks bewildered at Dad. Dad stares intently at the floor as if he's looking for an escape route. Miss is whispering, 'I'm sorry, I'm sorry . . .' Ali stands deflated now she's dropped her bombshell, like a stupid misguided suicide terrorist whose device has failed to go off. Only hers has and it's blown us all to smithereens. Tears stream down her face. She touches me.

'Jess?'

'Piss off!' I shrug her away.

'You'd better go,' says Carly. Ali mumbles something that sounds like, 'It's not my fault,' and disappears through the front door.

'You too.' Miss Taylor's bright orange coat is hanging on the end of the stairs. Carly thrusts it into her hands. Miss takes one anguished look in Dad's direction but he's still fascinated by the kitchen floor tiles. She turns to go but she can't manage the door catch. Carly helps her with it and holds the door wide open.

'Thanks.' It sounds wrong.

The door closes.

'Thanks.' Mum echoes Miss Taylor's words. She sits down heavily. 'Oh, Rob, what have you done?'

There's an ugly, raucous sound. Twice. It's Dad. He's sobbing. I've never seen Dad cry, not even at my nana's funeral.

I can't stand it. I wail, 'Mum! Dad!'

Carly comes over and puts her arm round me. 'Come on, kiddo,' she says, 'let's leave them to it.'

I want to say that the row rages all night then in the

morning I come down from bed and Mum and Dad are wrapped in each other's arms, with Mum explaining, 'This has made our relationship stronger than ever.'

No, I want to say, I wake up in the morning to find that this has all been a nightmare, like the one I used to have when I was little and a robber climbed through my bedroom window and asked me to marry him. I used to climb into bed with Mum while Dad went into my bedroom to shoo the robber away.

I want to snuggle into bed with Mum and Dad where it's all warm and safe and no bad luck can touch me, because I'm sick of bad luck in this family.

Only Dad's been to bed with Miss Taylor.

I can't go there. Not yet.

Actually, there isn't a big row. That's the strange thing. There's certainly a lot of talking because I can hear Mum and Dad on and off into the night, but the next day he drives her off to chemo as usual. She's white as a sheet when she comes back, but she always is. She goes off to bed and later on Dad takes her some soup.

She comes down to watch telly in the evening. She looks awful.

'Are you all right, Mum?'

'Don't bother your Mum, Jess,' says Dad. 'She's not feeling too good.'

I give him a stinking look. 'Funny that.'

'I'm fine, Jess,' says Mum. 'Don't worry. This chemo's really doing its stuff. Halfway through now.'

She's got deep shadows under her eyes. I hate my dad.

But at the same time I'm terrified I'm going to lose him. I'm afraid he's going to walk out of the door one day straight into Cathy Taylor's arms and set up his own little love nest. Then they'll have kids of their own and he'll forget all about me.

Shit.

How did all this happen? Where have the Boring Baylisses gone? I'd give anything to go back to Mum moaning to me about eating properly and Dad telling me off because my skirt's too short. Instead, my health fanatic mother is puking her guts up with chemotherapy and my decent, upright father has pulled my English teacher.

Guess what? I don't even tell Muggs what's happened. Do you know why? Three reasons.

1. Muggs thinks Dad is the best thing since sliced bread and I want it to remain that way.
2. It's embarrassing.
3. If I don't talk about the situation, it will go away.

And so, as the days pass and nothing happens, the status quo is preserved as Miss Taylor would say. (God, I can't help quoting the witch, even now.) I'm scared to ask if everything's okay. I'm even afraid to talk about it with Carly in case I bring back the cloud of malevolence that's been hovering over this family ever since I took on the role of Lady Macbeth.

Carly tries to speak to me one day. She comes into my room where I'm huddled under the covers and plonks herself down on my bed.

'Look, it may not be as bad as we think.'

My face is pressed into the pillows. I don't bother to lift it.

'What? You think it's okay for my dad to shag my teacher?'

'That's the point, silly. We don't know if he is shagging her, do we?'

'No, maybe they've been comparing achievement scores, or discussing scene changes for *Macbeth*,' I mutter sarcastically.

'Look at me!'

I raise my head and groan, then turn over and sit up against the pillows.

Carly looks as miserable as I feel.

'What?'

'We don't know if it was a full-blown affair, do we? I

mean, it might just be a snogging session that Ali walked in on. Think about it.'

Dad snogging Miss Taylor? Gross. Why would I want to think about that?

'Get lost, Carly. I don't want to talk about it.'

'Fair enough. But get it in perspective, Jess. We all do daft things. Maybe she led him on. Maybe it's the male menopause. Maybe she's trying to improve her promotion prospects! Who knows! But all we know for sure is Ali caught them snogging. So what? Big deal!'

I want to believe her. More than anything in the world. So I push aside those prickly little memories that Carly knows nothing about: Dad coming home late, Dad on the phone in the early hours of the morning, Dad disappearing for the day when he's supposed to be in school doing the timetable. And I say as casually as I can, as if I'm bored to death with the whole topic, 'Yeah, yeah, whatever,' and pretend to go back to sleep, much to Carly's annoyance.

Because the truth is, I'm terrified, and even though life seems to be going on as normal (whatever normal is, I don't know any more,) I can't get out of my head the sound of Dad sobbing and Miss Taylor's stricken little voice saying, 'I'm sorry, I'm sorry.'

And it's as if we're all frightened of each other, that if any of us say or do the wrong thing, our family will really fall apart once and for all. We're all tiptoeing around each other, with me being nice to Mum, and Carly being 'understanding' to us all, and Dad being quiet and sad and Mum being . . . quiet and sick. And it's doing my head in.

So when Gran comes to stay for her annual holiday, it's a fantastic relief. She arrives causing mayhem as usual, in a taxi, having caught an earlier train than expected, leaving Dad stranded at the station waiting for her. Mum had tried to put her off coming, but she wasn't having any of it.

'I've come to be useful,' she explains, extricating herself from the taxi, with a goldfish bowl tilting alarmingly under one arm, a collection of handbags under the other and a cigarette dangling from her lips. 'You won't have to do a thing now I'm here. Pay the taxi, Diane, would you? I can't reach my purse. Take these for me, girls.'

She waves at two huge cases the bemused taxi driver is struggling to get out of the boot. Cigarette ash drops into the goldfish bowl. The goldfish wisely swims out of the way.

'What's with the goldfish, Gran?' asks Carly, giving her a hug and trying to avoid the red lipsticky kiss being vaguely aimed in her direction. It lands on me instead.

'Neighbours away. The Maldives. Couldn't leave the poor little blighter on his own. Especially as I don't know how long I'll be away.'

She sails into the house, talking non-stop. The look of horror on Mum's face starts Carly and me giggling. When she mutters, 'Lord, save me from my mother,' we collapse into gales of laughter.

It's good to have Gran here. She's like a bit of comic relief in this horrible Shakespearean tragedy of a summer we're having. She reminds me of one of those terrible drivers, who drive blindly through life saying, 'I've never had an accident,' but leave a trail of debris and destruction in their wake.

She's determined to help. She's going to cook, clean, shop and wash for all of us and single-handedly nurse her only daughter back to full health.

Forget Jamie Oliver. She's from the 'Britain in the Blitz' school of cookery. So suddenly we're treated to fry-ups, roasts, sticky puddings, cake and, best of all, white bread and butter, neither of which has darkened our door for years. She genuinely believes that 'good food' will cure anything and when Mum protests weakly that she's trying to follow a meat-free, fruit and veg-based, dairy-free diet, she says, 'Good idea,' and serves her up steak and kidney pie and a home-made puff pastry apple tart with a big dollop of clotted cream. Which Mum eats up.

Carly and I quickly decide to do our own washing after Carly's Urban Stone dress and my new season H&M tops are returned to us two sizes smaller and a fetching shade of grey. Dad does his own ironing once his best silk shirt is given a new crinkle effect after being ironed within an inch of its life.

'Can't you stop her, Mum?' I protest, holding up my shrivelled hoodie.

Mum raises her eyebrows. 'Could you ever imagine me stopping my mother from doing anything? Anyway, perhaps there's method in her madness.'

'What do you mean?'

'Well, you're all doing a lot more round the house than you've ever done before.'

It's true. Dad's taken over the weekly shop to save Gran humping bag-loads of potatoes and flour home from town. Carly and I are doing the hoovering ever since Gran decided to tackle our rooms without her glasses on and vacuumed up two pairs of earrings, a set of false eyelashes and my geography essay.

And Mum's looking better, even though she's still in the middle of chemo. Maybe it's her mum's home-cooking; maybe it's because the atmosphere in the house is lighter, if more frenetic, now Gran's whirling round inside it. But actually, I think it's because of her amazing new hairstyle.

Can you call it a hairstyle if there's no hair? I suppose not. Mum's shaved her head and it's all Gran's doing. Well, hers and Carly's. You see, for weeks, Mum's hair has been getting thinner and thinner until you can see the scalp through it. She's been carefully combing what's left over the bare patches. She looks like Bobby Charlton and it doesn't fool anyone.

So one night while we're all watching *EastEnders* except for Gran who thinks it's too depressing, Gran says, out of the blue, 'Diane, why don't you shave your head?'

Dad looks alarmed. Mum's more interested in what's happening in Albert Square so she just says. 'I can't do that, Mum. I'm too old.'

Gran sighs. 'Ever the conformist! Of course you're not. It suits Carly. It would suit you.'

'It would Mum.' Carly sits up. 'Go on, let me do it for you.'

'I don't know. What do you think, Jess?'

'Go for it!' I smile at Mum. I don't believe she'll do it for a minute.

'It can't look worse than it does now,' says Gran with her usual tact.

That decides it for Mum.

'What the hell! Get the clippers, Carly. I'm going for a number one!'

In fact, she goes for the Full Monty. Carly finishes it off with Dad's wet razor. Then she does her own again, to keep Mum company.

They look great, more like sisters than mother and

daughter. It's weird, when Mum was trying to hang on to her hair and it was all grey and wispy, she looked old and ill and tired, but now she's shaved it all off she looks cool. Different, but cool. Her eyes look huge, especially when Carly outlines them with the special kohl she brought back from Thailand. She puts on the dangly earrings Dad bought her for their twentieth wedding anniversary at Easter and grins at him.

'Okay?'

'Beautiful,' he says, grinning back. I want to cry.

'You next,' she says, brandishing the clippers. 'You haven't got much to lose.'

'After you, Jess,' says Dad looking nervous.

'No way,' I protest. I'm not that brave. Muggs would do his nut.

'I will!'

'No, Gran!' we all say together and burst out laughing. Good old Gran, she's made us feel like a family again.

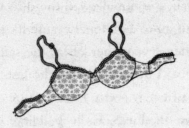

For a time, things seem to get to back to normal.

Mum seems to be tolerating the chemo better. Debbie comes round one day carrying a big bunch of sunflowers and a beauty box and squeals, 'I love your hair!'

'You mean you love my head,' says Mum wryly, but she lets Debbie give her a facial and a manicure and they chat for ages.

As Debbie goes she calls up the stairs, 'Ali would love to see you, Jess,' and I call back, 'Yeah, I'll give her a ring.'

But I know I won't. It's not that I blame her for what's happened. It's just that I know she'll ask me about Mum and Dad and Miss Taylor and I don't want to talk about it. I just want to forget it ever happened.

Carly gets an e-mail to say American Jake is in London and she wants to go to see him.

Mum says, 'Fine, just make sure you're back in time to get ready for uni.'

And you know, I don't start ranting and raving about how it's not fair, *I'm* not allowed to go to Cornwall and *she's* allowed to go to London, because it's not important any more. When I wave her off at the station with her backpack again, I'm not jealous, honest. Because the thing is, daft as it may seem, I need to be at home now to keep an eye on things. To keep an eye on Mum and Dad. To keep constantly on guard so nothing else awful happens . . .

You see, I've worked it out: we've been jinxed and it's my fault. I mean, I know it's not as simple as that, cause and effect. But the fact is, ever since I took the part of Lady Macbeth, we've had nothing but disaster.

So do you know what I find myself doing? You know those funny little rituals you do when you're a kid to ward off bad things happening? Like, you don't get into bed without looking under it, not because you think there's an axe murderer lurking beneath it, but because if you take the trouble to look then you'll be safe all night. I find myself doing stuff like that. For instance, I count in my head and if I can get up to fifty before Gran speaks, Mum won't die. I keep having to restart all the time because she talks so much.

I start touching the picture in the hall for luck before I go out so that Mum and Dad will still be together when I get back. One day I forget and I let myself back in with my key to touch it, and just as I'm going again, I see Gran staring at me. I say something like, 'I forgot my phone,' but I can tell she's not fooled and I feel stupid but I can't stop.

And then it gets that these tricks are not enough and I'm afraid to let Mum and Dad out of my sight at all. I can't bear it when Dad goes out on his own in case he's seeing Miss Taylor. I can't understand why Mum doesn't put two and two together and insist on going with him. She doesn't seem bothered.

One day she scares the life out of me.

'Where's Dad?' I ask. Mum's on the sofa watching *Countdown* with Gran.

'Gone to see Miss Taylor,' she answers absently. My heart does one of those wild leaps and dives into the pit of my stomach.

'I've got five,' says Gran. 'What about you?'

'Six,' says Mum. ' "Heresy".'

'Very good,' says Gran admiringly. 'I've got "Sheer".' She looks at me standing there gawping at Mum with all the wind knocked out of me. 'What's up, Jess?'

Mum looks up. Why doesn't she care? Why isn't she daubing the trollop's house with words like 'WHORE!' and 'BITCH!' instead of making anagrams with Carol Vorderman.

She looks puzzled momentarily then bursts out, 'Oh,

it's okay, Jess. They're just sorting out this flipping school trip.'

My heart starts to climb back up to its rightful place. She seems okay with this, even though I can see this could be just another excuse.

'Don't look like that! He's not up to anything. He's only nipped out for half an hour.'

She sounds amused. Her attention moves back to the television but Gran's watching me, concerned.

'Is he still going, then?'

'Well, that's what he's trying to sort out. If they can't find anyone else daft enough to take twenty-odd kids to a rock festival in the middle of their well-earned summer holidays, then I guess he'll have to.'

'Don't you mind?' Can't she see what's going on in front of her eyes?

'Not really,' she says coolly. 'Not as much as you do, obviously.'

And it turns out Dad does go because Mum's right, no other teacher in the whole of the school wants to accompany the cast of *Macbeth* to Cornwall at the end of August.

The night before they leave I feel sick. Muggs and I go to the cinema, the only place we can get some peace to be on our own without his kid brothers and sisters or my gran popping up. Muggs is feeling amorous, probably because he knows he won't see me for a week.

'I wish you were coming,' he says, taking the opportunity of the darkness and the nearly empty cinema to pull me close. 'I don't want to go without you,' he whispers. I can feel his breath, toothpaste clean, on my cheek and his hand gently massaging my shoulder.

'Don't go, then,' I reply, calling his bluff. I grin in the darkness as Muggs's hand stops in mid-stroke.

'Do you mean it? I mean, I won't if you really don't want me to. Ali doesn't want to go any more either, I was talking to her last night. If you . . .'

I put him out of his misery.

'It's okay, you go off and play ghoulies and ghosties with your mates in Cornwall. I'll stay home and learn my lines. I don't mind, honest.'

Truthfully, I don't. Well, not in the way he thinks, anyway. I should be mad as hell at not being allowed to go away with my bloke and my best bud and loads of other mates to a rock festival organised by my favourite teacher. But I'm not. That's history. Okay, I'm not exactly over the moon at being left behind, but it's just not my priority any more.

Because things have changed so much.

For a start, *she's* my most *un*favourite teacher now. No, my most unfavourite person. I don't even like saying her name. I still don't know how I'm going to face her when we go back to school, let alone have lessons and rehearsals with her. Weird, it's as if *I've* done something wrong, not her. *She* should be afraid to face *me*. Perhaps she is.

And I'm not talking to my best bud these days.

Plus, the biggy. I don't know how I feel about Muggs any more. I've not gone off him, no way. I still think he's drop-dead gorgeous. But I'm happy just being with him, having a laugh, holding hands, snogging, that sort of thing and, to be absolutely honest, I'm not ready for anything else. Not yet.

That's the trouble really. Part of me knows Mum's right. You see, what would happen in Cornwall with everyone else on the pull? If I'm with Muggs 24/7 could I trust myself? Like my head might say NO! but my body might let me down and scream YES!

And the thing is, my sex life (or lack of it) is just about the only thing I am in control of nowadays.

Maybe a week apart will be the best thing all round.

Anyway, I've got to keep an eye on Mum. I've just got this horrible feeling in the pit of my stomach that things are going to get worse.

Question: What could be worse than your mum having breast cancer and your dad having an affair with your teacher?

Answer: Your mum dying.

Mind you, I don't tell anyone how I feel. I just act cool and noble about being left behind and let them all feel guilty. Dad can hardly look me in the eye when he's getting ready. It's obvious he doesn't want to go. He gives Mum and me a peck on the cheek at the front door and says, 'See you in a week's time.' Mum says, 'Be good,' and he looks as if he wants to take her in his arms and give her a big bear hug, but she closes the door. When we turn around Gran is watching us.

'You don't miss a trick, do you?' says Mum and goes into the kitchen.

I go up to school to wave Muggs off anyway, even though I won't walk up with Dad. I feel a pang, I have to admit, when I see everyone milling round with their sleeping bags and tents, clutching copies of *Macbeth*. Muggs holds me close as if he'll never let me go and even Jade says, 'Wish you were coming, Jess,' though Kelly throws her a filthy look.

Then Ali comes up to me and gives me a hug and I have to swallow hard like there's a giant-size frog taking up residence in my throat when she whispers, 'Don't worry, I'll keep an eye on things for you.'

And I know she means it by the look she stabs at Miss who's counting people on to the bus. There's no way they can get up to anything with Ali on guard. And if I keep a beady eye on Mum, well, between us we'll keep the curse of *Macbeth* away from my family's door.

The last thing I see as the bus goes off is Ali waving like mad out of the back and Kelly shifting her bag to sit by Muggs. Bitch. I don't care. Muggs is my one constant in an unstable world. He won't let me down.

When I get home, Gran must have been bending Mum's ear about me and my funny goings-on because Mum asks me if anything's wrong.

'Wrong? What could possibly be wrong? No, I just love the fact that I'm at home with my mother and grandmother while my boyfriend, my best mate and the whole cast of the play in which I happen to be the leading lady have gone off to a music festival without me.'

I could have continued with, 'in the company of my father and his bit of stuff,' but that would have been too cruel. Anyway, as Miss says (oh blast, I'm doing it again), irony is best served light.

Mum studies me carefully.

'I thought you'd come to terms with it. Look, Jess, I don't want you to think you've done anything wrong. I mean, you don't have to hang around the house, you're not grounded. Go out and enjoy yourself, you don't have to be stuck in with Gran and me.'

Poor Mum. She hasn't a clue what's going on in my mind. I feel like Lady Macduff's son left to protect his mother while his father goes off to fight evil Macbeth. Their conversation echoes through my mind:

'Was my father a traitor, mother?'

'Ay, that he was.'

'What is a traitor?'

'Why, one that swears and lies.'

'And be all traitors that do so?'

'Every one that does so is a traitor and must be hanged.'

'And must they all be hanged that swear and lie?'

'Every one.'

But it's not the traitor, Macduff, who deserted his wife and child, who dies, is it? It's poor, innocent Lady Macduff and her son. So I have to keep watch over Mum in case . . . in case something terrible happens to her.

I tell you what, I'm becoming an authority on this play, I've studied it so hard. I reckon I could go on *Mastermind* and do *Macbeth* as my specialist subject. The more I read it, the more similarities I can see with what's going on in my own life.

Perhaps I'm becoming obsessed. Perhaps I'm going

mad like Lady Macbeth? I certainly feel as if I'm losing it. I take myself off to my bedroom and pick up my script. Might as well become word-perfect.

When Mum goes to chemo next, she asks me if I want to go with her.

'What for?'

'I don't know. Just to see what's goes on, I guess. Though it's not very exciting.'

This makes me feel better. Because I imagine it as something of a torture chamber where you're strapped down and poisonous substances are injected into you against your will. We learned about the Holocaust in Second World War history and the image of Hitler's extermination camps are in my mind. The truth can't be worse than my imagination.

'All right, then.'

'Good. Gail's husband's picking me up because your dad's not here to give me a lift. I'm sure there'll be room in the car.'

So that's how I find myself sitting in the back of a people carrier entertaining nine-month-old Alfie while Mum and Gail chat away nineteen-to-the-dozen in the middle and Steve chauffeurs us to St John's.

And, you know something, it's not a bit like I expected. I thought it would be full of old, really sick people, but it's not. I mean there are a lot of old people but there's also young ones like me, and little kids as well, though they go into a separate room and all their nurses are dressed up like clowns or nursery rhyme characters. Mum and Gail are greeted like long-lost friends and the first thing Mum does is go over to a fridge standing in the corner of the room and help herself to a Magnum each for her and Gail out of the freezer compartment.

'Sorry, Jess, not for you. We need them to keep our mouths cold during treatment.'

Yeah, sure. Gail has to share hers with Alfie who doesn't buy this feeble explanation. Then a rather gorgeous male nurse called Paul comes to take charge of Mum and explains to me that freezing the inside of the mouth helps to prevent ulcers from forming. He chats to Mum all the time the treatment is taking place. She has to have three drugs, but he puts a canula into her hand so she only has one injection. It's all over in twenty minutes and Mum looks relieved.

Poor old Gail is having a harder time of it. Her nurse has trouble getting the needle into her hand. She tries her arm, then calls another nurse for assistance. A bowl of hot water is brought to soak Gail's hand and arm and eventually the second nurse manages to insert the canula in her wrist. Gail's face is white.

That's not the end of her ordeal. She's determined to keep her hair so she's still having the cold–cap treatment which Mum abandoned when she shaved her head. This means she's in the chair for nearly three hours wearing a kind of ice-cold bike helmet. Mum explains the cap is maintained at minus 30 degrees to freeze the hair follicles before, during and after treatment, so the drugs don't affect them at their most toxic stage and the hair shafts are preserved. Gail sits, frozen and uncomfortable.

When Mum is finished we take Alfie off in his pushchair to the café and leave Gail with Steve. I glance back at her as we leave the room. Steve is rubbing her hands to make her warm, taking care not to dislodge the canula. A nurse brings her a blanket. She looks exhausted.

'Are you okay, Mum?' I ask in the café. I get to give Alfie a bottle, which is really cool. He stops sucking and gives me a big milky grin.

'I'm fine, love,' she says, taking a sip of her tea. 'Ooh, I needed that. I'm just a bit tired now. I'll sleep tonight.'

'. . . the innocent sleep,
Sleep that knits up the ravelled sleeve of care,
The death of each day's life, sore labour's bath . . .'

Macbeth's words flit in and out of my mind. They're becoming an inner voice that threatens to overtake my own thoughts. It's like I'm leading two parallel lives, one in eleventh-century Scotland and one in the twenty-first century, each moving along its own tracks, aware of each other all the time. I'm scared stiff one day they'll collide.

I feel a gentle, soothing touch, midway between a pat and a stroke, on my face. I look down. Alfie is patting my cheek as he sucks rhythmically on his bottle. He pauses and stares at me intently. A bubble forms at the side of his mouth. He lets out a huge contented fart and beams with delight.

'Aah,' Mum and I say simultaneously and we both burst out laughing.

Dad phones every night at 7pm, before *EastEnders* or *Corrie*. Muggs phones and texts all the time. They're having a ball. Though he's careful not to say this. He says the bands aren't up to much and the weather's iffy. And he's missing me like mad. I believe him.

But they're working hard on the play, he says, especially the army scenes, because they've got loads of space to amass the soldiers and see who needs to go where. Apparently, my dad's ace at choreographing the marches and the battle scenes. Hidden talents!

I'm not in those scenes so I'm not missing anything. I'm dead and buried by then. Not that Macbeth seems to care.

'She should have died hereafter.'

That's all he has to say when he hears of my death, me, his *'dearest partner of greatness'*, his *'dearest love'*. Men!

He's been totally corrupted and prefers to spend his time dabbling in the black arts with the weird sisters than looking after his poor, sad wife who's going quietly mad back home in her lonely castle.

Life repeating art again! Here am I, stuck at home, while Muggs makes music with those *filthy hags'*, Kelly, Jade and Ali, in not-so-sunny Cornwall.

Actually, I'm not quite as cool as I'd like to be about this. Think about it. I mean, Miss wants them to play the witches as vamps who tempt Macbeth with their sexual charms. Huh! She should know! Well, that's right up Kelly's street, isn't it? I know damn well she'd do anything in her power to get Muggs to succumb to her unearthly pleasures.

Nah, get a grip. I trust him. And anyway, Ali's keeping an eye on things, isn't she?

'Jess?'

Lady Macbeth and I are in my bedroom again, going over our last big scene. She's sleepwalking and though her eyes are open, *'their sense are shut'*. It strikes me that's my normal condition nowadays. She's barking mad now, beset by demons of guilt and darkness. Not much trace left of the feisty control freak from Act 1. Getting her own way hasn't made her happy.

'Jess!'

I'm lost in thought on how to deliver the *'Out damn spot'* line. It's a really poignant part of the play but, if I'm not careful, everyone will titter at the thought of a little Labrador pup with a patch over his eye coming in where he's not wanted. So Gran's voice makes me jump a mile. She's standing at my door looking at me curiously.

'You were away with the fairies.'

'With the witches,' I say, showing her the text.

'You spend too much time with your head in that book.'

'It's not a book, Gran, it's a play.'

'You know what I mean. Your mum's gone to see Gail. Can I come in?'

She plonks herself down on my bed and takes off her slipper to massage her bunion. 'Ooh, that's better.'

It's been good having Gran around.

'Are you coming to see the play, Gran?'

'I should do, the time you and your dad have spent on it.'

I glance at her. Her face gives nothing away. How much does she know about what's been going on?

'Do you want to be an actress when you leave school?' Gran asks, plumping up my pillow and making herself comfortable.

Do you know, that's something I've never considered, strange as it may seem.

'I don't know. I've always assumed I'd go to uni.'

'Like Carly?'

'Yeah, I guess so.'

'But, you're not Carly.'

'I know. But, I mean, it's always been taken for granted that I'd go and do something like English or History, subjects I'm good at.'

'You're good at acting. Anyone can see that.' She picks up my framed photo of Muggs. 'Nice-looking boy. He needs a haircut though. He'd have been called a sissy in my day, wearing a ponytail.'

'It's fashion, Gran.' I giggle at the thought of Muggs, captain of the school rugby team, being branded a 'sissy'.

'Taken for granted by whom?'

It's hard sometimes keeping up with Gran's thought processes. They make detours.

'Oh, I see. Mum and Dad, I suppose.'

'Hmm. You're just like your mum.'

'What?' What is she on about? 'Mum doesn't like acting.'

'She used to. Anyway, I don't mean in that way.'

I put down my book and look at Gran. 'In what way, then?'

Gran puts down the photo of Muggs and picks up the one of Mum and Dad by my bed. She traces the outline of Mum's face with her finger. Her face is soft.

'She could have done anything with her life, your mum. She was so talented.'

'Like me, you mean?' I smile brightly at her. She stares at me seriously.

'Yes. But, even more like you, she was always afraid of taking the plunge.'

I need a translator. It suddenly crosses my mind that maybe she's sussed out what Muggs and I are up to. God, is my grandmother encouraging me to have sex? How embarrassing! I feel my cheeks warm.

'I mean she always spent her life doing what other people expected of her. Doing the right thing. Didn't get her anywhere, did it?'

Thank goodness, it's not the birds and the bees she's on about. Then I think about what she's just said. She makes it sound as if Mum's had a terrible life.

'She's happy,' I protest. (Well, she was before cancer struck and Dad's brains descended into his trousers.)

'Yes, of course she is. She thinks the world of you and Carly. She'd do anything for you.'

And Dad, I say in my head. Say Dad as well.

'But that's just it,' she continues, warming to her subject. 'She's spent a lifetime pleasing other people.'

'What do you mean?' As far as I can see, Mum's always done exactly what she wanted. She certainly calls the shots in this family.

'Well, for instance, she married your dad because she was expecting Carly and he wanted her to.'

'Did she?' I stare at Gran aghast. I didn't know Mum was pregnant with Carly before she got married. I suppose I could have worked it out if I'd ever given it any thought. I wonder if she felt about Dad the way I feel about Muggs, then push that thought quickly out of my mind. Mum and Dad having the hots for each other – yuck!

'Then she trained as a teacher because your granddad said she'd be good at it. She was too, she worked so hard at it, just like she worked hard to be a good wife and mother. But I don't know . . .'

'What?' This is important. I've never thought of Mum having to work hard at being a wife and a teacher. Or a mum, especially a mum. I thought it all came naturally.

'Somewhere along the line that little free spirit got lost. Somewhere in a mire of work and domesticity. She had so much potential. She could have been anything: a writer . . . or an artist . . . or a dancer . . .'

'Gran!' She's talking about Mum as if she's dead. When she looks at me, there are tears in her blue eyes. Or maybe they're just rheumy, like old people's.

'She should have sown a few wild oats, had a bit of fun.' She sees my expression and says, 'Sorry, Jess, I shouldn't go on so much. Take no notice. I'm just a daft old woman.'

She knows.

She knows about Dad and Miss Taylor. And she's not judging them. She just wishes it had been her little girl who had the affair.

I put my arms around her waist and bury my head in her ample bosom. She strokes my hair.

'You youngsters,' she says fondly, 'I forget you're so conventional.'

I look up at her. 'You're an old floozy, Gran.'

She smiles. 'I think you're right, Jess. A silly old tart. Your mum would go mad if she thought I was talking to you like this. But, promise me something?' She puts her fingers under my chin and lifts my face to hers.

'Anything.'

'Don't let other people dictate your life, Jess. Be yourself, not what someone else wants you to be. Promise?'

'Promise.'

Only it's too late. I've already become someone else. I'm Lady Macbeth. And I'm scared stiff because her life doesn't end happily.

Then suddenly our crisis summer is over.

Dad's home. He walks in carrying a strong-smelling carrier bag full of ripening Cornish pasties which Mum immediately disposes of in the bin in spite of Dad's protests. She looks reasonably pleased to see him though and he does his usual hug and pat on the back routine.

And Muggs is sooo pleased to see me.

'I missed you so much,' he says, squeezing me as if he'll never let me go. He's brought me a lovely necklace made out of tin, mined from deep beneath the Cornish sea. Eat your heart out, Kelly, you old hag.

'You look knackered.' His eyes have shadows under them and he seems tired and subdued.

'Too much to drink last night,' he confesses. 'Party on the beach till the early hours. Wish I hadn't bothered now.'

'Can't take the pace,' I jeer at him, gently. 'The alcohol ban worked, then. And where was my dad in all this?'

'Slept through it all.'

Hmm. Makes a change for Dad to have the wool pulled over his eyes.

Gran leaves on the train in a maelstrom of suitcases and carrier bags. She forgets the goldfish. As we wave her out of sight, Mum says, 'Alleluia!' but she wipes away tears surreptitiously.

'Gran's cool.' I link my arm with Mum's as we walk to the car.

'Yes, she is,' she admits in surprise. 'Do you know, I never thought the day would come when I'd be sorry to see my mother leave.'

She and Gran have definitely become closer over these past weeks. Mum's changed. She's more relaxed now she's stopped being Superwoman and juggling her career with her family. Weird, how things turn out. I glance at her. Did she really settle for second-best, marrying Dad? Has her life with us been a disappointment? God, I hope not!

And then it's back to school and there's a flurry of shirts and shoes shopping, and pens and paper and brightly coloured files to buy, and books and assignments to locate from where they were dropped and forgotten six weeks ago. Good. I'm glad the summer's over and I can go back to holding hands with Muggs at break time and netball training and the precinct after school – and THE PLAY!

Because sod Miss Taylor and her designs on my dad. It was a waste of time. She hadn't reckoned on the strength of the Bayliss family ties, no way. So now she can go back to doing what she's good at, which is teaching English and directing plays. I'm mature enough to deal with this.

Mind you, just to make sure, the first thing I do when I go back to school is grab Ali and pull her to one side.

'So?'

'What?'

'Did he behave himself?'

'Who?' She looks alarmed.

'Who do you think? Duh! My dad, of course. You said you'd keep an eye on him, remember?'

'Oh, yeah, sure. They never went near each other except for rehearsals.'

'Good. What about you?'

'What about me?' Why is she so jumpy?

'What did you get up to? God, you're hard work today.'

'Oh, nothing. Just the play. It was all right, nothing special. You didn't miss a thing.'

And it seems as if she's right because if it was a bonding exercise it's failed. Okay, they've got the second half of the play sorted out which is the tricky boring bit (because I'm not in it much, ha ha) but it's weird. Everyone seems edgy, maybe because the play takes place in three weeks' time and we're all getting a bit apprehensive.

I thought Ali would be big buddies with Kelly and Jade, but that's not the case. In fact, she seems to be the butt of their bitchiness now, with Kelly making sly comments to Jade when she's around. Obviously she's done a good job of keeping an eye on Kelly's antics, as well as Dad's, and it's wound Kelly up. Good old Ali.

Anyway, it doesn't make for good rehearsals with the First and Second Witches glued together at the hip and the Third Witch looking a bit unstuck. But it works in the scene where Macbeth goes back to visit the witches because all of them now seem to hate him with a vengeance. Kelly does a superb job, even though I hate to admit it, of playing with him as if she's got something on him. Even Ali looks as if she hates his guts. The air crackles with tension.

Miss goes into ecstasies.

'Well done, you witches. Where did that come from? There's a real edge to your acting now.'

Kelly looks smug. Miss continues.

'Now, this is the part in the play where you really commit to evil, Macbeth. From now on, there's no trace of Mr Nice Guy, you are corrupt.'

'You can say that again,' remarks Kelly. Jade hoots. Miss looks nonplussed.

'Is there something I should know?'

'No, Miss, nothing *you* should know,' says Kelly.

She's getting on everyone's nerves. Muggs looks as if he could wring her neck, Ali gives her a look of pure hatred and Liam who plays Macduff says, 'Then shut it, Kelly, and let's get on with the play.'

For a moment it's as if there's live static in the room which is going to set off a huge explosion, then Kelly turns on her heel and marches off.

'Bitch,' says Muggs, voicing what's in everyone's mind. I'm not stupid, I know what she's trying to do, but I won't fall for it. Because I know my boyfriend better than that and I can tell by the tone of his voice that he would never go near that evil witch no matter how many spells she cast.

And Muggs and I are brilliant. The first scenes are a doddle because basically they're love scenes where I use my sexual power to get Macbeth to do what I want. I know this woman backwards and I know how much she loves her husband and wants what she thinks is the best for him. It's easy to do this with Muggs whom I love (I think) so I just go for it and Muggs responds and it's ace.

'That's excellent, Jess,' says Miss. 'Well done, you two.'

She looks me in the eye for the first time since that awful day. I manage a small smile.

'Thanks.'

I can do this. It's going to be all right. I can work with her on a professional basis.

If the first scenes are easy, the banquet scene is tougher as I desperately try to cover up for Macbeth who gives the game away that he's a murderer. This is hard to play. You see, Lady Macbeth actively encourages Macbeth to kill Duncan, but doesn't bargain on the fact that he gets a taste for blood and then goes off on an orgy of murder without telling her. You can see why it's a brilliant play and even the boys in my class who think literature's for poofters like studying it.

But from my perspective, I have to play it so that,

1. this powerful, manipulative woman slowly realises her control over the love of her life, and indeed, her life itself, is heading down the pan, and

2. I have to get the audience to feel sorry
    for her, even though they hate her for
    getting Macbeth to kill good King
    Duncan.

Difficult. But not impossible. And you know how I do
it? Life imitating art again. I've been practising this. I
thought about how confused and shocked and sad I was
when I found out Dad had been playing away, and all the
things I wanted to say to him and was afraid to in case he
left for good. I summon up all those feelings again and
take out my frustration and fear on Macbeth, spitting out
lines like,

'Are you a man?'

and,

'Shame itself!'

and,

'What, quite unmanned in folly?'

and,

'Fie, for shame,'

with all the bitterness and disgust that still lies within me.

There's a name for this type of acting, you know. We
did it in drama. It's called method acting and it's based on
a character's inner motivation. Well, what motivates me is

my anger at Dad for letting us all down. Lady Macbeth and I have a lot in common. We both know what's it like to be dumped on by the man you love.

It's very effective. I know, because there's a silence when the scene is over and then everyone says, 'Wow!' and 'Amazing!' and 'Go, Jess!' even though it's really Macbeth's scene. Sorry, Muggs, I've upstaged you.

And Miss looks at me and says, 'That came from somewhere deep inside you.'

And I say, 'Yeah, it did,' and stare straight back at her but she can't meet my eyes and turns away.

It's tonight. The first night. It's come at last. Four months of blood, sweat and tears. We're nervous as hell.

Last week we were all word-perfect. Today we can't even remember when to come on! We had a crap dress rehearsal and no one knew their lines. The witches were dreadful, you couldn't hear Malcolm, the Porter didn't raise a titter and the scenery fell down. Even Macbeth missed an entrance!

'Not to worry,' says Miss, looking as if she wants to cut her throat. 'A bad dress rehearsal is a good omen.'

Huh!

The play's a sell-out. No wonder; Muggs has got all his family coming to see him, not just Dee and Ron and their brood, but his real dad and his wife and kids. They take up the first two rows. I've never seen him so excited.

It's good to see him back to his old self. Ever since he got back from Big Rock he's been quiet, as if there's something on his mind. Mind you, we haven't had much chance to be alone together, what with rehearsals every night and coursework piling up now Muggs is in Year 11. I know he's dead keen to do well at GCSEs. He told me he wants to be the first person in his family to get to university.

Actually, I've got a few fans coming myself tonight. Carly's back from London and is packing to go off to Bristol next week for Fresher's Week, so she'll be there. Gran's arriving this afternoon and Mum's bought tickets for them all plus Gail, who really has become her bosom buddy. It's cool, I can't remember Mum having a friend before: I guess she was too busy. Anyway, she and Dad were always best mates.

Dad'll be backstage doing the scenery and props. He's nearly as nervous as I am. I've had a chance to keep a close eye on him and Miss Taylor over the past three weeks and I can honestly say I've not noticed anything going on between them. They're just like two colleagues who get on and work well together, which is all they are, thank God. Carly was right. A male menopausal blip. Silly old Dad. I feel a sudden pang of sympathy for poor misguided Miss Taylor, who fell victim to Dad's doubtful charms, and stick a pound in the collection for her bouquet when Jade comes round rattling the tin.

And talking of flowers, guess what? When I get back

to school this evening ('Six o'clock sharp, don't be late,' Miss warns us), I've got my own bouquet waiting for me in the drama room. I've never had one before. It's a dozen red roses and lots of that white gypsum stuff, all done up in cellophane.

'*To my Leading Lady*', is written on the card. I feel like a star.

Muggs is watching me anxiously. I fling my arms around him.

'I love you!' I shriek.

'I love you too,' he says quietly. He sounds so serious as if he's confirming it to himself. 'Don't you forget it.'

'As if,' I say, propping them up against the mirror so I (and everyone else) can see them as I'm doing my make-up.

Kelly's face is a picture. She's jealous as hell. I've got loads of good luck cards to open too, whereas she's only got one, and that's one of those sent jointly by Muggs and me to the rest of the cast. She doesn't even thank me when she opens it and she stuffs it back in the envelope instead of putting it out on the table like everyone else.

'Now scat.' I give him a kiss. 'I want to get changed.'

We're doing it in modern dress, twenty-first-century fashion. Miss's idea. The witches look tarty as hell: Kelly's in tight black leather trousers and bomber jacket with sleek gelled hair; Jade's wearing a boob tube and miniskirt with fishnet tights, wild hair and huge hooped earrings; Ali's in torn hipster jeans and a plunging neckline, blonde hair piled on top of her head, escaping from its clasp, bejewelled belly button on display. They're wild, aggressive and predatory. Whereas I look . . . classy.

I'm wearing a slinky, deep blue dress in a soft, shiny silk, which accentuates my curves without being too tight. My hair is pulled back into a sort of chignon. It emphasises my cheekbones and the line of my neck. The neckline is low and my collarbones stand out (I've never noticed them before!). The material falls softly round my breasts, drawing attention to them before curving and clinging to my stomach (flat, thank goodness) and my hips. I have on stilettos that throw my bottom out provocatively and make my legs look as if they go on for ever.

I look different, much older and sexier, in a far more subtle way than the witches. No wonder Macbeth finds me irresistible!

Mind you, he's quite tasty too. He's wearing a white dinner jacket with a black silk shirt, black tight trousers and black shiny shoes. And to link him with me visually, a silk tie of the same deep blue as my dress. What a couple! We should be at the Brit Awards.

Someone from the local paper comes to take our photo and we pose together, arms wrapped round each other. Kelly's lurking in the background and the photographer asks her to get out of the picture.

I catch the expression on her face. She's livid.

The atmosphere builds up in the drama room. Jade frets because her tights have a hole in them but Miss says it adds to the effect so she makes another hole in the other leg and Miss tells her off. The girls angst about their costumes and make-up while the boys worry about forgetting their lines. The soldiers are told to line up their swords against the wall until it's time to go on before someone's stabbed to death.

People peep out of the drama room door to see if their mums and dads have arrived, though Miss has expressly forbidden us to do so. Mrs Shepherd comes along to wish us luck and tells us the hall is packed and there's standing room only.

And before we know it we're ready to go. Miss moves us into the centre of the drama room and we form a circle and hold hands. All involved in the play join in: cast, backstage staff, make-up, costume people, everyone. I see Dad coming in and Ali makes room for him in the circle and takes his hand. He smiles at her and she grins back. I feel choked.

Then, with Miss leading us, we start quietly repeating the words,

'Two, four, six, eight,
We will not equivocate.
Macbeth's about to meet his fate,
We're the cast and we are GREAT!'

172

Slowly the pace and intensity of the chant builds up. It becomes loud, vibrant, enormous, filling the room with its pulsating rhythm, making us one. Miss signals us to bring it to a huge triumphant halt and we cheer and hug each other. Then silence, broken by whispered 'Good Lucks' and admonitions to 'Break a leg!' as we line up ready to take our places backstage.

And we're on! Heavy metal music, jarring and strident, heralds the arrival of the weird sisters on stage. There's a momentary giggle from the audience at their appearance and then the play begins with the rising and falling of the witches' voices as they start spinning their web of deceit and intrigue.

The audience is brilliant. They love it. When Muggs and Banquo walk on in Act 1, Scene 3, wolf whistles and catcalls of approval greet them. And, the old pro that he is, Muggs waits for them to calm down before he speaks his line, linking him to the witches.

'So foul and fair a day I have not seen.'

And they're hooked. It's going well. Kind old Duncan, played by Ryan from Year 11, gets the audience to warm to him . . . and then it's the turn of Lady Macbeth. Someone pats my shoulder as I wait in the wings for my cue.

'Good luck, Jess.'

I turn. It's Miss. Impulsively, I squeeze her hand. She looks astonished and grateful at the same time. I don't have time to dwell on it because I'm on.

I step on to the stage, my husband's letter clutched in my hand, and do you know what I hear? A gasp. It comes from the fourth row down on the left-hand side and I know who it is. It's Mum.

And guess what? Everyone starts clapping before I've even said anything. And I take my cue from Muggs and wait till they've finished. Then I begin.

I read Macbeth's letter aloud to the audience. We see what the witches have promised him, that one day he'll be King. I confess my fears to them. He's *Too full o'th'milk of human kindness To catch the nearest way.*

He will have to be persuaded to kill good King Duncan. But I'm not as wicked as I make out. I have to call on evil spirits to help me. It's the *Come to my woman's breasts* speech from my audition and I milk it for all it is worth. I'm no stereotype wicked queen: I'm a full-blooded, passionate, ambitious, loving wife, using the only power I have to get what I want.

I was born to this role.

Muggs has to wait in the wings for his entrance because the audience cheers and applauds at the end of the speech. And then, finally, we're together on stage and I'm so genuinely pleased to see him I run to him and we kiss. He picks me up and spins me round and we laugh and all the audience says, 'Aahh!' and we laugh again because none of this is scripted, it's completely spontaneous. The audience loves us, we've got them in the palms of our hands, and slowly the story starts unfolding to its inevitable tragic conclusion.

The interval falls at the end of the banquet scene. It's a key scene, a major turning point in the play. From this point on, Macbeth will stop at nothing in his relentless rise to power and he abandons me, his remorseful, useless wife. At the interval, Miss is in raptures.

'It's going so well,' she repeats. 'Well done, all of you. That was brilliant, Jess and David.'

I shine with joy. I feel as if Muggs and I are caught in a spotlight of success and happiness. I can't wait for the second half.

'*Will* you close that door, Kelly!' shouts Miss. Kelly's being her most annoying, holding the door open to talk to members of the audience as they go to collect their glasses of wine from the canteen.

'Sorry, Miss. Just admiring Jess's mum's new hairstyle. The cancer crew cut. Very fetching.' She giggles.

The drama room falls silent.

Then Ali says, 'You cow.'

Kelly looks around. Ali's voiced what everyone's thinking. Even Jade looks embarrassed. Kelly knows she's gone too far. Her eyes narrow.

'Me . . . *you're* calling *me* a cow?'

'Watch it, Kelly,' warns Liam.

'*She's* got the cheek to call *me* a cow?' she repeats.

Ali is watching her transfixed, like a rabbit caught in the headlights of a car.

'Just leave it, Kelly,' says Muggs. He's white, tense. A pulse throbs in the side of his forehead.

What the hell is going on?

'At least I don't get off with other people's boyfriends!'

Not from want of trying, I think to myself. What's Ali been up to? I thought she was still going out with Sean.

'You don't get it, do you?' Kelly glares at me. No, I don't. I look around. Ali is crying. I look at Muggs.

He says, 'I'm sorry, Jess. It wasn't like that.'

Oh no.

Oh please, no.

He's betrayed me.

And it wasn't with Kelly.

It was with Ali.

Ali rushes out.

Kelly mutters, 'Shame you had to find out this way. But someone needed to tell you.'

'Be quiet, Kelly. You've said more than enough already.' Miss puts her hand on my arm. 'Jess?'

'Don't touch me,' I snap. She snatches her hand away quickly as if she's been burned. I stare at Muggs. He looks as devastated as I feel.

'It wasn't like that,' he repeats.

'Is she making it up?'

'No, I'm bloody well not,' screeched Kelly. 'That little tart had it away with your precious boyfriend on the beach at Big Rock!'

Tell me it's not true. Please tell me it's not true.

Muggs is shaking his head. What does that mean? I look at the faces of the rest of the cast. They look embarrassed. No one will look at me. I feel exposed, raw, naked.

I hear this dreadful, ugly sob emerge from deep inside me and I run out of the door, away from those awful sorry-for-me faces. In the corridor the audience are milling round with glasses of wine, chatting about the play. I catch sight of Mum and Carly in conversation with Mrs Shepherd. Mum's smiling modestly as if she's basking in my success. Then she spots me and her smile fades.

Carly catches up with me in the loo, briefed by Miss Taylor, who can see her beloved play collapsing before her eyes. I'm wrecked. I cling to my sister as I gulp air in between the huge, racking sobs that tear me apart. She holds me tight and gradually I stop crying, though my body still shudders with huge convulsive sighs.

'I look a mess.'

There's no trace left in the mirror of the sophisticated and beautiful Lady Macbeth. My hair has worked itself out of the chignon and is hanging down in straggles. Mascara has run in two black lines down my cheeks and make-up is smeared all over my face. My eyes are red and puffy.

I look like a woman betrayed. Which I am.

Through the door comes the sound of heavy metal music again. The play has restarted. Kelly's getting it in the ear on stage from Hecate, the Queen of the witches, for messing with Macbeth. Hecate's words come floating through:

'And which is worse, all you have done
Hath been but for a wayward son,
Spiteful and wrathful, who, as others do,
Loves for his own ends, not for you.'

How true is that? Yet it's not quite right, is it? It was the Third Witch, not the First, who had her wicked way with him. I missed that one completely. I should have seen it coming.

'Jess? Are you okay? You're on in a minute.' Carly's looking at me with concern.

'I can't . . .' Tears threaten to engulf me again.

'Yes, you can.' Mum's standing at the door, eyes huge with concern. I reach out to her and she folds me in her arms and I sob again.

After a while, she moves back, then holds me by the shoulders at arms' length and looks into my eyes. 'Your dad's told me what happened. It's awful. We need to talk about this, Jess, but not now. Now you've got to finish the play.'

'But, Mum, I feel . . .'

'I know how you feel! Believe me, I've been there.'

'Oh, Mum,' I sob. Of course she does. If anyone knows what I'm going through it's her. 'I don't know which is worse, Muggs or Ali.'

'I know. They've both let you down big time. But that

doesn't mean you have to behave the same way. There are five hundred people out there who can't wait to see what happens to Lady Macbeth. Some of them have never seen a Shakespeare play before. They love it! You were brilliant in the first half, Jess. You've got them hanging on every word. Don't let them down.'

She's right. Why should I let Muggs and Ali steal my moment of thunder from me? Gran's words float into my head: *Don't let other people dictate your life for you, Jess.*

I blow my nose hard. I'm surrounded by wise women in my family with their own kind of spells. I smile weakly at Mum and Carly and see the relief on their faces.

They slip into the darkness of the auditorium and I take up my position backstage ready for my cue, ignoring everyone. Miss is so relieved she tries to pat me, remembers how her last attempt ended and her hand flaps about in mid-air. She converts it to a thumbs-up sign and says, 'You're a trouper.'

And I go out there and give the performance of my life as poor, sad, mad Lady Macbeth. If this is method acting, then I'll get the Oscar. (Do they have Oscars in the theatre?) Because *I am* the woman betrayed. I don't need make-up. I look the part in a way that my vanity would never have allowed me to look normally, with tumbled hair and ravaged face. I have become Lady Macbeth.

I can feel the sympathy exuding from the audience as Lady Macbeth and I wander the stage together. We're two tortured souls, racked with grief at the way life turns out in spite of our attempts to control it. We wring our hands together and sigh from the depths of our souls.

You see, we thought we were invincible, each one of us part of a golden couple: Macbeth and Lady Macbeth; David Morgan and Jessica Bayliss. Nothing could hurt us. Huh! Pride comes before a fall, so they say, and now we girls have been dumped, like last week's rubbish. Life's a bitch. And we know there's nothing we can do about it because our very last words to each other are:

'What's done cannot be undone.'

We've got to move on, but will we make it? Well, I know *she* won't, my sister in sadness. But, will I? Tears pour down my cheeks as I abandon her for ever.

When I move off stage, Miss Taylor is crying too.

Guess what? I get a standing ovation at the end. Muggs and I have to come on together holding hands after the rest of the cast and crew is assembled on the stage. I do it. I hold his hand. The audience claps and cheers us like mad. Then Muggs leads me into the centre of the stage and drops my hand and joins in the clapping and all the audience, every single person in it, gets up on their feet and applauds me. Dad steps forward and holds my hand in the air.

'I'm so proud of you,' he says and kisses my hand. I feel like a queen. Then he points to my lovely, crazy family. Carly is whistling and yelling, clapping her hands above her head and stamping her feet. Mum is crying. And Gran has clambered on to her seat and is waving her scarf in the air as if she's at a football match and shouting, 'Encore! Encore!'

And you know something? No one, not poisonous Kelly, not treacherous Ali, not Muggs or Dad and their stupid, horrid little flings, not even bloody cancer, can take away the glory of this moment from me.

It's magic.

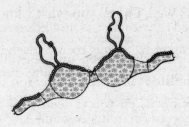

The Epilogue

I know what you're thinking. You want to know what happens next. Tie all the loose ends up. Shakespeare did this in some of his plays. It's known as an epilogue. There isn't one in *Macbeth*.

Perhaps he didn't believe in happy endings any more. I don't either.

So, what do you want to know? Let me guess.

You want to know if I went under like poor old Lady Macbeth.

You want to know if Muggs did have it away with Ali and if it's all over between us.

You want to know if Ali and I are still mates.

You want to know if Dad's affair with Miss Taylor is really finished and if Mum and Dad are still together.

You want to know if Mum survives breast cancer.

Am I right? Well, I'll tell you what I know myself. It's not much.

No, of course I didn't pop my clogs like Lady M. I didn't contemplate it for one minute. You don't consider suicide an option when you've seen your mum battling hard to stay alive.

I've stopped the superstitious rituals too. They don't work.

Muggs and I are still together. Sort of. I'll never really know what happened in Cornwall. He says he was missing me like mad and feeling horny. On the last night he got pissed at the party and ended up on the sand dunes with Ali.

She says she was lonely without Sean, but admits she was fed up with playing second fiddle to me and thought (under the influence of a fair number of alcopops) she'd see how far she could get with my boyfriend.

They reckon they didn't actually do it. Do I believe them? Yeah, of course I do, otherwise I wouldn't still be going out with Muggs. It's not the same, though. Not yet. Maybe it never will be. Anyway, he's off to college next autumn.

Ali and I still go down the precinct together. Oh, and she still copies my work. I'll never trust her again, but she's still Ali. Scatty Ali.

Carly's having a ball at Bristol. I don't know if she's actually made it to any lectures yet, but she's certainly working her way through the new male intake. I'm going to stay with her next weekend, sample the university scene. Consumer research.

Mum's invited Gran to stay with us for Christmas. Gran's not sure if she can make it. She's booked to go to Las Vegas with the over-60s club.

I'm working hard for my GCSEs. I suppose I don't need them if I'm going to be an actress (now Gran's planted the idea in my mind) but I want to keep my options open. Anyway, it's not easy to break the habit of a lifetime.

Mum's finished her chemo. She has radiotherapy now, every day for six weeks. It's a doddle, she reckons, compared to chemo. She and Gail go together and take in a bit of retail therapy or cappuccino society afterwards.

When their treatment's finished, they're going to throw a party. She never mentions going back to school, but she did say the other night that, when all this is over, perhaps she should do something different. Apparently, she's always wanted to be a writer.

Mum reckons cancer's given her the opportunity for change. She says Dad didn't mess about with Miss Taylor because she was ill. Their marriage was 'tired' anyway. So, what's wrong with tired? Tired is warm and comfortable,

I argue. No, she replies. Tired is worn-out and draining.

Because, this is the hardest thing to say: Dad's left. He's not moved in with Miss Taylor, he's living in a flat round the corner from school. I call in most days for a cuppa on my way home.

I couldn't believe it when Mum and Dad told me. Together, of course. A trial separation, they said, while they work things out. Why can't they have a trial staying together?

I thought it *was* all worked out. I thought Miss Taylor was history. Perhaps she is. I hope so.

Time will tell. I guess if you want a happy ending to this story you're going to have to write your own.

I don't blame 'The Unlucky Play' for all that's happened any more. I mean, it's like Mum says, it's not what life throws at you that's important, it's how you pick up the pieces afterwards.

By the way, we've already decided, next year we're having a change from Shakespeare. We're going to put on *Grease* instead. And guess what part I'm going for? No, not Sandy, no way. She's too bland and boring. I'm going for the battle-scarred Rizzo. Much more interesting.

She's a survivor. Like me.